"Don't you ever think of me?" Danny asked softly

The closer he got to her, the crazier it drove her. It was his scent. In fact, she'd once said yes to a date with a man she wasn't even remotely interested in just because he smelled like Danny Rodriguez.

"Nope," Celia said, trying hard not to show she was lying.

"Not even a little bit?" He moved closer.

Danny leaned over and planted his hands on the chair's arms. He was close. Too close...

"Really? Because I still think of you...all the damn time."

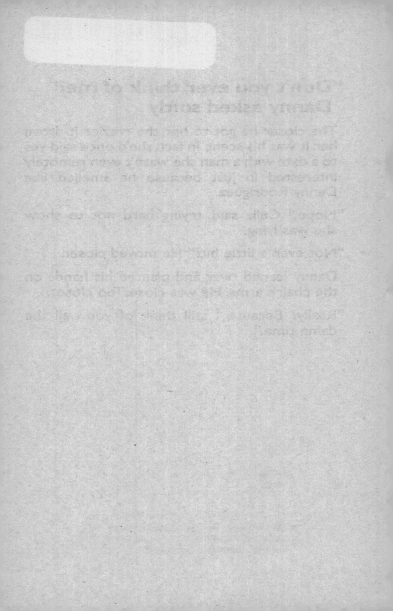

"Don't you ever think of that?" Danny asked softly.

The closer he got to her the weaker it flowed her. It was his scent. In fact, she'd once said yes to a date with a man she wasn't even remotely interested in just because he smelled like Danny Rodriguez.

"Nope," Calla said, trying hard not to show she was lying.

"Not even a little bit?" He moved closer.

Danny leaned over and placed his hands on the chair's arms. He was close. Too close.

"Really? Because I will think of you all the damn time."

NEXT OF KIN
TRACY MONTOYA

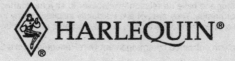

HARLEQUIN®

TORONTO • NEW YORK • LONDON
AMSTERDAM • PARIS • SYDNEY • HAMBURG
STOCKHOLM • ATHENS • TOKYO • MILAN • MADRID
PRAGUE • WARSAW • BUDAPEST • AUCKLAND

ISBN 0-373-88657-8

NEXT OF KIN

www.eHarlequin.com

Printed in U.S.A.

ABOUT THE AUTHOR

Tracy Montoya lives with a psychotic cat, a lovable yet daft Lhasa apso and a husband who's turned their home into the Island of Lost/Broken/Strange-Looking Antiques. A member of the National Association of Hispanic Journalists and the Society of Environmental Journalists, Tracy has written about everything from Booker Prize—winning poet Martín Espada to socially responsible mutual funds to soap opera summits. Her articles have appeared in a variety of publications, such as *Hope, Utne Reader, Satya, YES!, Natural Home* and *New York Naturally*. Prior to launching her journalism career, she taught in an underresourced school in Louisiana through the AmeriCorps Teach for America program.

Tracy holds a master's degree in English literature from Boston College and a B.A. in the same from St. Mary's University. When she's not writing, she likes to scuba dive, forget to go to kickboxing class, wallow in bed with a good book, or get out her new guitar with a group of friends and pretend she's Suzanne Vega.

She loves to hear from readers. E-mail TracyMontoya@aol.com or visit www.tracymontoya.com.

Books by Tracy Montoya

HARLEQUIN INTRIGUE
750—MAXIMUM SECURITY
877—HOUSE OF SECRETS*
883—NEXT OF KIN*

*Mission: Family

CAST OF CHARACTERS

Celia Viramontes—Years have passed since her now-deceased lawyer father defended young gang members involved in a teenaged girl's death. Now that someone wants revenge, will Celia allow her ex-boyfriend Daniel Rodriguez to keep her safe?

Daniel Rodriguez—A detective with the LAPD's elite Homicide Special unit, Daniel takes a leave of absence to protect his ex-girlfriend Celia from a killer. But will old feelings cause her to refuse his protection and drive a wedge between them for good?

Sonia Sanchez—Years ago, she was murdered during a gang-related initiation rite, and her brother Marco vowed revenge on all involved.

Marco Sanchez—When his sister died, he swore to go after the nine men involved, as well as the lawyer who set seven of the nine free—and his family.

Patricio Rodriguez—Proven innocent in Sonia Sanchez's murder, ex-gangbanger Patricio, Daniel's twin brother, has lived for years with the guilt of not being able to prevent Sonia's death.

Francisco Sanchez—Marco's brother is also still angry about the death of his younger sister.

Maribel Sanchez—Marco and Francisco's downtrodden mother. She tries her best to keep her sons out of trouble.

Joe Lopez—Daniel and Patricio's oldest brother, recently reunited with them after a long separation.

Lola Ibarra—Daniel's Homicide Special partner. The senior detective keeps Daniel informed about the Marco Sanchez case.

Chapter One

No matter how many times Celia Viramontes flicked the switch up and down, the storage room lights refused to go on.

Which wasn't really a big deal—it's not like she was afraid of the dark or anything—but there was that *smell*.

She brought her hand up to cover her mouth and nose, her chest heaving as her body rebelled against the sticky, cloying odor of something big and burnt. She'd never liked the smell of burnt anything— her neighbor's penchant for starting bonfires of fall leaves in his backyard nearly drove her to drink. Even a too-sooty candle was enough to send her retching in the opposite direction.

But *this*. This was her worst olfactory nightmare.

Celia turned and dashed up the basement stairs as fast as her Jimmy Choos would carry her. Pushing through the steel door, she heaved herself into the main lobby of St. Xavier University's Thomas More Library, the domain over which she had presided for the past several years. Only a hint of that terrible, terrible smell hung in the air up here, as the heavy gunmetal-gray door with its tiny window of wired safety glass did an excellent job of blocking most of it. Not that there was anyone else who would notice. She'd shooed out the last few students at 10:00 p.m. and had just been going through the various rooms to ensure there weren't any stragglers before she closed the building down for the night.

Her eyes swept the lobby, barely registering the neat stacks of magazines in their wire carousels, the day's newspapers piled by the double glass doors for recycling pickup, the gleaming hardcovers showcased face-out on shelves with a laminated

New Books! sign hanging over them. But though she still had miles to go before the library was ready for tomorrow's students and she could go home, Celia found herself having an internal debate over what to do about The Stench. Check it out? Ignore it and hope it would go away? Blitz-attack it with an industrial-size can of air freshener?

Spinning on her black stiletto heels— not the utmost in comfort but so cute she couldn't resist wearing them to school at least once a month—she headed for the front desk, hitting its half-door full stride. The wood panel smacked against her thighs and swung back on well-oiled hinges, swinging back and forth behind her as she headed for the supply cabinet under the desk's computer terminal. Dropping to a crouch, Celia rummaged through the cabinet until her hand closed around the solid black metal handle of a flashlight that could probably double as a weapon. It was her only nod to personal security since Oscar Valencia, the muscle-bound custodian who took care of her library, insisted on walking her to her car every night.

But she hadn't seen Oscar since... *Dios mío.*

Since he'd pushed his industrial-strength mop and wheeled bucket into the elevator and headed for the basement storage room more than two hours ago.

"Cut it o-o-o-out. You're being a drama que-e-een," Celia singsonged under her breath as she clutched the heavy flashlight. She threaded her way back through the card-catalog computer terminals toward the stairs.

And then, for no apparent reason, her feet refused to take her any farther.

Her eyes focused on the stairwell door next to the wheelchair-access elevator, but, for the life of her, she couldn't make herself take another step. A terrible fear at what lay beyond wrapped itself around her ankles and traveled up her body with pointed, prickly fingers.

You listen to your intuition, Celia Inez, her mother had always told her. *It might save your life someday.*

Celia took a step backward.

The near-monastic silence of the library

swept over her like a gentle yet terrifying tidal wave. And, heaven help her, the burning smell seemed to have gotten stronger despite the steel-and-safety-glass barrier.

"Go forward, just go forward," she muttered. It was probably a squirrel that had taken a wrong turn out of the quad, the stretch in the middle of the small campus of grass and pathways leading to every major building. And here she was, turning a dead squirrel in her storage room into the Southern California Chainsaw Massacre. She willed herself to move down the stairs.

Her body twitched in the right direction and then did an about-face to the front desk of its own accord. She ran back where she'd come from, heaving her midsection over the counter until her feet dangled off the ground. Her fingers closed around the heavy receiver of the standard-issue telephone that plagued every office and lobby at St. X in a stubborn affront to interior decorators everywhere. Pulling the receiver to her ear, she punched in the number for Campus Security—conveniently the same number as Campus Information—and waited.

"'Lo, St. X info desk. Hah-meh-hep-yoo," a sleepy female student answered.

Enunciate much? Celia thought to herself, but instead said, "Can you please send Security to the library?"

"Wha?" the voice answered.

"Security!" Celia snapped, recognizing and hating the fear in her voice. "I need Security!"

"Okay, whatever. You don't have to shout," the student responded with about as much feeling as a toadstool. "Whassa problem?"

"It's—" Celia began and then stopped herself. A smell. *That's great, Cel. Tell her all about the big, bad smell that's putting you in mortal danger.* How in the world would she be able to face the 1,350 students and faculty members of this fishbowl of a university if everyone found out she'd called Security in a panic over a *smell?* "You know what?" she said, putting on a slight French accent in a perfect imitation of Dr. Chevalier, the French professor who never brought her books back on time. "It is—how you say?—no big deal. I am fine. *Merci* buckets." She couldn't put the receiver back in its cradle fast enough.

With that, the chilling silence of the library enveloped her once more, reminding her that unless Oscar was playing hide-and-seek with himself amid the basement study carrels, she was totally alone. Okay. What to do now? She could lock the library, leave for home and hope that the smell would sort itself out on its own during the night. She could go downstairs with the flashlight and show herself how ridiculous she was being by facing the probable dead squirrel head-on. Or she could sit here all night and grow increasingly paranoid until the psych department students took her away for observation and closer study.

Celia picked up the flashlight from where she had set it on the counter and smacked the head against the palm of her free hand. Ignoring the smell and hoping it would go away seemed to be the most attractive option, but she'd be damned if she was going to be a girlie girl who couldn't handle a dead squirrel. She headed once more for the stairs.

Reaching the stairwell door once more, she gripped the heavy knob with her free hand and twisted, nearly gagging at the thick stench that wafted out to greet her. The charred odor made Celia feel as if she'd tried to swallow a piece of burnt toast, leaving her esophagus scratched and coated with ash. Coughing softly into her hand, she made her way through the small basement study area and opened the door to the storage area. Immediately, the smell grew even stronger—an occurrence she hadn't thought possible until experiencing it—and she was enveloped in darkness. Celia pressed the soft plastic coating covering the flashlight's on button, and a beam of warm yellow light pierced the darkness. Better, but not by much.

Space in the long, narrow room was mainly occupied by a maze of industrial metal shelves containing piles of old books and equipment that needed to be repaired or donated. She waved the flashlight beam around, illuminating pieces of shelving, boxes of books that had just come in, a collection of ancient computers coated with grime, airborne dust bunnies...

And a dark figure lying in the middle of the shelf maze.

That wasn't a squirrel. That was Squirrelzilla.

Celia jerked the flashlight beam from left to right in an erratic attempt to brighten every square inch of the room. She felt only a small measure of relief when she realized no one else was in there with her. At least, as far as she could tell. There was always the boiler room tucked in the far right corner.

Don't think about the boiler room in the far right corner.

Doing her best to clear her mind, Celia took a deep breath—which she immediately regretted as it sent her into a coughing fit—and stumbled toward the figure. Her thin and pointed heels clicked on the concrete floor. The burning odor grew thicker and more cloying in her nostrils and throat. Her breathing seemed to become louder and louder, until it and her heartbeat were the only sounds she could hear. And then, finally, there was only one long series of shelves between her and the…thing on the floor.

She tiptoed to the end of the row of shelves, the gray metal bars blocking a new piece of the mysterious form every time she glanced back at it. Finally, she turned slowly around the corner, trailing her fingers on the dusty metal, and headed for the figure with nothing between her and it but darkness.

Just as she reached whatever it was, her foot connected with something soft, and she nearly stumbled on top of the thing. It was longer than she'd expected. Clutching the shelves with her free hand for support, she aimed her flashlight at the floor. The beam illuminated a heavy brown shoe, with a clunky rubber sole that would have made it a good choice for hiking. The kind Oscar Valencia always wore.

Celia breathed in. She breathed out.

And she prayed that time would stop so she didn't have to see whatever lay before her.

Feeling as if she'd been submerged underwater, Celia let go of the metal bracket she'd been clinging to with an agonizing slowness, her flashlight beam bouncing off the ceiling. She lowered it.

Directly onto what looked like a charred log. With an identical charred log lying next to it. The beam traveled up, to where the logs joined together to form one big trunk. To a piece of blue cotton, black at the edges, stuck to the main body. To a flash of white bone. To a withered black hand with curled, clawlike fingers.

To a pair of wide-open, lidless eyes.

She heard a scraping sound behind her, steel against concrete. She wasn't alone.

"Celia," a voice whispered behind her in the darkness.

THE ST. XAVIER UNIVERSITY library was already blocked off with yellow crime-scene tape by the time Detectives Daniel Rodriguez and Dolores "Lola" Ibarra of the Los

Angeles Police Department's Homicide Special unit arrived on the scene.

Every LAPD bureau had its own set of homicide detectives, and normally the West Bureau would have sent its people to the scene. But when Captain Aaron Mulvaney, the chief of Robbery and Homicide Special, had found out that the crime had taken place at a university that counted the mayor's daughter and the governor's son among its student body, he'd immediately told his detectives to get their asses over to St. Xavier. The elite Homicide Special unit of the LAPD's top detectives had a long and distinguished history of taking on the city's most high-profile cases—from the Robert Kennedy assassination to O.J. Simpson to the Night Stalker—and now the St. X. homicide was all theirs.

Gre-e-e-eat.

As Daniel cut his way alongside Lola across the damp, spongy grass of the St. X quad, he had a very bad feeling about this homicide, this case, this crime scene. Then again, that might have had more to do with the location than anything else. God help him if you-know-who had been on library duty tonight....

Beside him, Lola stopped abruptly, shoving her hands into the pockets of her ancient gray trench coat. She looked a little like someone's schlumpy aunt with her permed short hair shot through with streaks of gray, a permanent slouch, and what had to be the ugliest glasses he'd ever seen post-1977.

"Hey, Junior," she said. A seasoned investigator with years of cracking cases under her belt, Lola usually called all new Homicide Special detectives "Junior," Danny had been told, until they proved they had what it took to last among the LAPD's "best of the best." Even though he'd spent one year with the unit and had been through two partners, Lola hadn't let up yet.

"Why don't you go get an update from McManus?" Lola continued. Officer Carrie McManus had been the first officer on the scene, and as such, had most likely already collected preliminary statements from the reporting party and any witnesses. "I'll talk to the EMTs, and then I'm going inside." The last was tossed over Lola's shoulder, as she'd already started ambling toward the flashing red lights as if she hadn't a care in the world.

"Sure," Daniel murmured absently, his attention riveted on the library doors and the woman he imagined could step through them at any moment.

Man, this was seriously going to suck, unless Lady Luck was with him tonight. But something in his bones told him she'd taken the nearest bus out of Dodge.

Daniel ducked under the tape perimeter and headed across the concrete path, figuring that the cluster of people around the library's front entrance was as good a place as any to find the officer. Turned out, he was right on target. McManus stood under a security lamp, which leached most of the color out of her square-jawed face. She scribbled furiously into a small notebook while a young woman talked animatedly to her, her hands fluttering about her face in extravagant gestures.

He knew those gestures.

Not to mention that crazy, curly hair and inexplicable love for flamboyant shoes. Celia Inez Viramontes, St. X's head librarian and the woman who'd broken his heart.

But it was your choice, doofus, the little voice inside his head reminded him.

Yeah, whatever. He'd had no choice at the time. It had been either pay attention to his girl or save his brother's life, and no one had had to tell him twice which option had been the best one.

But then why, for the love of God, did it still hurt to look at her after eleven years?

Clenching his jaw so tightly he thought his teeth might break, Daniel pushed himself forward, until he was within eye- and earshot of McManus and...dude. That wasn't Celia.

Idiota. With that sharp nose and slight overbite, the girl couldn't have looked less like Celia from the front. Not to mention that Celia had at least half a foot on her when it came to height, with legs that went on for days. And...okay, thinking about

Celia's legs as they had looked a decade ago was not productive. He quashed the image in his head and tuned into what the woman was saying.

"So Jerry and I walked by," the-woman-who-wasn't-Celia said to McManus. "Jerry's the guy I was on security escort duty with, who called you—and the library door was, like, wide open. That's *so* not normal, because Dr. Viramontes would be all 'grrrrr' if someone stole or defaced one of her books." She curled her fingers into claws at the "grrrrr." Oh, yeah, she knew Celia, all right.

Daniel waited while the student, who worked the occasional security shift escorting lone students from one end of campus to the other, finished her tale of finding the library door open, finding a badly burned body—male, he knew from Mulvaney's account—in the basement, and, most important, finding Celia.

"Is she all right?" he asked abruptly. Both the student and McManus turned to look at him, McManus's ice-blue eyes narrowing in question. So maybe that came out a little more concerned than it should have. He stared back, giving them both what his twin brother liked to call his Badass Cop Look—the blank, no-nonsense one he used in the interrogation room while playing bad cop. Not that Ibarra let him play bad cop very often, telling him that with "that honest face," he practically had a sign on his forehead proclaiming him "pushover cop" to all who entered Robbery and Homicide's station doors. But sometimes he could sweet-talk her into it.

Stepping closer to the student, he conveyed his silent "Well?" with a tilt of his head and a lift of his eyebrows. The girl shrank back a little and lifted her arm to point at a spot directly behind him. "She's in there. You can ask her."

Relief that Celia was alive and well made his heart skip a beat.

Or maybe it was just panic at the thought of seeing her again.

Not yet. Fortunately, McManus complied with his unspoken wish to postpone the inevitable by sending the young woman away and flipping back a few pages in her notebook. "We've got a definite homicide in the basement, sir," she began. "The head librarian, a Dr. Celia Viramontes, discovered the vic at 10:17 p.m. after heading down there to investigate a bad smell. Burn victim—we'll need to have the medical examiner ID him, though Viramontes seems pretty sure he's the building janitor. Smells like someone doused him with an accelerant and lit him up like a Christmas tree, sir. Poor guy. Based on the lack of burn marks at the scene, I think he was killed somewhere else and the body transported here."

Daniel swallowed his reflexive scowl and waited while McManus continued her macabre litany of information. She and her partner had been the only ones who'd entered the crime scene so far after the campus security guards who'd found Celia, and she'd kept it cleared, despite a few slippery reporters and impatient lab techs, until he and Lola had arrived.

"Nice job, Officer," he said, and she beamed. Before he could stop himself, he felt the corners of his own mouth turning up in an answering smile. Rookies.

"Thank you, sir. I'll have a copy of my report on your desk tomorrow morning."

He nodded and turned toward the library, and through the glass doors, he caught a glimpse of long legs in painful shoes; crazy, curly hair; and a mouth he remembered all too well—one that didn't show the slightest signs of an overbite. The vision of the real Celia was like a sucker punch to the chest. She was in a dark red pantsuit, with a brilliant orange tank that told him that despite the fancy degree and the high-pedigree job, his girl could still be funky.

She's not your girl, Chief.

He pushed the thought out of his head. All that mattered was getting to her, making sure she was all right. Because eleven years or not, no one was going to hurt Celia Viramontes without answering to him.

He shoved through the doors and into the library's well-lit lobby, stopping a few feet away from rows of computer terminals through which an obviously shaken

Celia was making her way, leaning slightly on a gangly paramedic who was probably responsible for the white patch of gauze taped to her forehead.

"Mild concussion," McManus supplied helpfully as she stepped up behind him. "Someone—possibly the killer—was still in the room when she found the victim's body, and he knocked her out before he escaped."

Daniel felt his gut twist at her words. It had been close. So close. One snap decision by a deranged mind, and Celia could have been killed instead of just injured.

"She said he called her by name before he left. Don't know what to make of that, sir," McManus said.

Daniel tucked the cop's words into the back of his mind, where he could take them out and turn them over and over later, searching for clues as to who killed the man who lay in the basement of the library. Right now, he didn't have time for anyone but Celia herself.

He knew the moment she recognized him. Because even though Celia had the most beautiful brown skin he'd ever seen, it could turn a scary shade of pale whenever she was angry. And Celia Viramontes could go from zero to angry faster than anyone he'd ever met.

"Dammit, Danny Rodriguez," she said quietly, "your ugly mug is the last thing I need to see right now."

And Daniel knew he was in trouble. Because even though a long time had passed since Celia had last spoken to him without using the words "jerk" and "flying leap off my universe," as well as a few choice Spanish phrases his mother used to wash his mouth out with soap for uttering, he still found himself wanting to tear apart the person who'd put that look of fear on her face.

Chapter Two

The terrifying thoughts that had flooded Celia's mind since she'd regained consciousness were abruptly drowned out by one shrill question: *What the hell is Danny Rodriguez doing here?* He looked better than a man had a right to look, dressed in a well-cut black suit with a charcoal-gray shirt and blue silk tie. With his close-cropped hair and his striking light brown eyes, he looked classic, expensive—but then, Danny could make faded jeans and a T-shirt look expensive. Whatever blend of quiet mystery, in-your-face presence and sheer hotness Gregory Peck and Cary Grant had had, Danny possessed it in spades. Damn him to everlasting misery.

More exhausted than she'd ever felt in her life, Celia let go of Steve-the-Paramedic and closed the space between her and her Emotionally Unavailable Jerk Ex-Boyfriend. Closed it, and then walked right past him to the front desk. She didn't have time for this right now, didn't have time for him. Ever.

What do I do? She squeezed her eyes tightly shut, trying to banish the images of what she'd seen once and for all. It didn't work. The image of the bones of a hand, the sweet hand that had closed softly around her elbow and guided her safely to her car every night for the past several years played against her eyelids in too-stark clarity. *Oscar, oh, poor Oscar. How could I not hear? Why didn't I get to you sooner?*

Danny cleared his throat behind her, apparently having followed her. "Celia?"

She spun around to face him, her hands clutching the scratchy brown blanket Steve-the-Paramedic had placed over her shoulders. And whatever shreds of an idea she'd had about ignoring him faded away as soon as the sheer weight of his presence slammed into her with an almost tangible force.

"What are you doing here?" she asked, and her grief over Oscar, over what he'd *suffered,* put more fury into her words than even Danny Rodriguez perhaps deserved. "What could you possibly have to say to me?" And, just as soon as the white-hot lightning bolt of her anger had hit, it was gone. She felt her body slump as all of her energy seemed to drain away. "Danny, who would do this?" she whispered.

He folded his arms, pulling his suit coat a little tighter across his broad shoulders, and shook his head. The few feet between them felt like an ocean. Celia swallowed and blinked, making a superhuman effort to hold back the tears that wanted to spill out of her. Danny wasn't good around tears or any kind of big emotion—he got all awkward and weird. And she didn't want to make him feel awkward; she just wanted him to go away.

"I don't know yet, but I'll find out," he replied. "I promise."

Yeah, and you promised to love me un-

til you died, you jerk, she thought, but for once, the words in her head didn't come shooting out of her mouth. He hadn't just broken her heart, he'd jumped on it, ground it into little tiny pieces under his shiny black cop shoes, and then flung the smashed remains into the nearest slime-ridden sewer drain. And there was no way she'd ever let him see how much he'd hurt her. Which is why she'd gone eleven years without speaking to him, and why she'd go eleven more after that. A decade-plus-one at a time, until one or both of them were gone.

She turned away from him, and a rebellious tear squeezed out of her eye and rolled down her cheek. Celia didn't know if it was only for Oscar or also for the girl she'd been at nineteen, when life was good, school took up most of her time, and Danny Rodriguez had been her whole world.

"Look." She swiped at her face, her back to him. "I've talked to I don't know how many officers here, and I really don't want to talk to you, too, so can whatever it is you want to say to me wait until tomorrow? Because right now, I'm going to lose it in a big, bad way if I have to go over what happened tonight one more time."

He sighed, and Celia had a moment where her heart rebelled and remembered a time when she had made Danny sigh like that, over and over and over again.

"Sorry, Celia," he said in his maddenly calm-and-collected cop tone, trilling her name with the correct Spanish pronunciation *Seh*-lee-ah instead of the anglicized *Seel*-yah that she hated. She knew there were only inches of space between them, and God, it wasn't enough. "We have to talk to you while everything's fresh in your head. But maybe I'll let Detective Ibarra do it," he said, in that same quiet voice that had haunted her for so long. "I'll see you." And then he turned away from her and headed toward the basement stairs.

She didn't move, didn't even blink. Count to ten, twenty, infinity until Danny Rodriguez was out of the room, out of the building, out of her life again. Count until she could breathe again.

I'll see you. Not again. Not ever, if she could help it.

AFTER SNAPPING ON A PAIR of latex gloves McManus had helpfully handed him, Daniel joined Lola in the basement shortly after she'd talked to Celia one last time and sent her home. Just as he was about to enter the room, he compartmentalized his thoughts, putting Celia neatly into a corner in the back of his mind. Because if he allowed himself one more minute to think about the smell of her perfume, her *curvas* in that figure-hugging red suit, the way her thick, curly hair used to feel under his fingers, he'd lose his mind. Then again, after only a few minutes of her company, maybe he already had.

Get out of my head, baby girl.

And with that, she was out, at least for the next few hours. He pushed through the door to the basement storage room and entered. Immediately, the sticky-sweet burnt smell overpowered him, and he broke into a hacking cough that seemed as if it would never end.

Lola peered at him over the rims of her Unabomber glasses. "Here you go, Junior." She tossed a small blue container of Mentholatum at him.

His fist snapped closed around the flying jar as his attention was drawn to the body on the ground, illuminated by a portable lantern Lola had placed on a nearby shelf. Ugh. Poor guy.

"Just so you know, it never gets any easier, seeing someone like that," Lola said through the shelves. She moved her flashlight beam back and forth, carefully walking in a gridlike pattern that would allow her to cover every square inch of the basement in her search for clues.

Knowing the drill, Daniel followed suit, starting from the other side of the room. Between the two of them, after a good solid two hours of searching, they came up with a cigarette butt smashed into the floor of the boiler room and a faint shoeprint in the dust and ashes around the body. Daniel bagged and tagged the cigarette stub and photographed the footprint. As Lola focused her flashlight on the dirt-strewn area, Danny took care to point his camera directly over the print after placing a small ruler from his pocket next to it for scale. The crime-scene analysts would undoubtedly photograph the print as well, before using electrostatic film to pick it up, but Homicide Special detectives liked to build in redundancy.

"Yo, Lola, no prints on the door, according to Jerry, our friendly neighborhood latent-print examiner. Can I come in now?" Dr. Apollonia "Polly" Singh poked her head through the door. Lola shone her flashlight directly into Polly's eyes, making the woman blink rapidly.

"Yeah, why not?" Lola droned, as if bored. Lola only droned when she was frustrated. Apparently, the gruesome murder was getting to her.

Stepping into the room, Polly pulled a pair of gloves out of the pocket of her white lab coat, snapping each at the wrist once she'd tugged them on. Under the coat, she wore a pair of jeans and a T-shirt, probably the first thing she'd found after being called away from her home late in the evening. Tyvek booties kept her from tracking trace from her shoes around the body, and the entire ensemble was topped off by a red *bindi* dot, placed carefully between her dark eyebrows. She bent down to examine the body, her diagonally cut bangs falling to partially shield her face as she focused on the victim's hands.

"Thought I'd try to get a set of prints off our guy here, in case he doesn't have dental records," she said matter-of-factly as she attempted to collect evidence from under the corpse's fingernails. Not that she was likely to get any, since the fire had probably burned most of it away.

"Polly, his hands are burnt to a crisp. You won't be able to—" Lola stopped abruptly, her pale skin turning even whiter in the dim light.

This time, Daniel didn't even try to hide his grimace. "Polly, you are one disgusting woman, you know?"

The medical examiner had actually peeled the skin off of the victim's one hand that still had skin—burnt and blackened though it was—and had stretched it like a second glove over her own latex-covered fingers. She pressed the fingertips into an inkpad and was rolling the entire mess onto a piece of white card stock.

"You just couldn't wait until we got him back to the lab, could you?" Lola said, a slight tightness in her voice.

"Now, you'd think so," Polly replied, intent on her gruesome task, "but I like to print burn victims before we move the body. Prevents things from crumbling or falling off and getting lost, ya know?" Polly blew her bangs out of her face and wagged her eyebrows at them. "Thanks for being here, you guys. This is always so much more fun with an audience."

"Nice," Daniel responded, crossing his arms and planting his feet. His foot connected with the metal structure behind him, causing a can of spray paint to rattle into view from under the bottom shelf. He ignored it. If Polly, that four-foot-nothing wisp of a woman, could take it, so could he—and he wasn't the one wearing a dead man's hand. And although he'd have gladly chewed off his right arm for another dose of Mentholatum under his nose, he wasn't about to give in and apply some more.

"Getting queasy, Detective Macho?" Polly asked, still trying to get a print.

"Nope," he said, sounding bored.

"You sure?" She wiggled the hand in the air. It made a soft smacking sound, the kind that his mother's lasagna made when you cut the first piece out of it.

"Yep." He yawned, covering his mouth with a fist.

"What you got, Singh?" Lola interrupted, still droning. Sometimes he just wanted to kiss Lola. Especially when she put an end to things that made him want to puke all over a crime scene.

"Think I got a couple of complete prints. We'll compare them to any that Jerry can get from this area and the janitorial closet—if you ever let him in," Polly said pointedly, "and see if we get a match with Oscar Valencia. We'll have the lab run them through AFIS, too." AFIS was the national Automated Fingerprint Identification System. If the victim had ever been arrested or worked for the government after the mid-1990s, his prints would be in there. Then she started talking about other ways she could try to get a positive ID on the body back at the morgue, but Danny barely took it in.

Spray paint.

Over the almost overpowering odor coming from the body, Daniel caught a slight whiff of what could have been fresh paint. Crouching down, he shone his light under the metal shelves until he found the spray paint can he'd kicked earlier. Swiping a gloved fingertip across the nozzle, he wasn't surprised when it came away with a smudge of fresh black paint.

Making a mental note to bag and tag the can in a minute, he set it down on one of the metal shelves and trailed his flashlight beam across the walls of the room—one, two, three—until he found what he was looking for on the fourth wall. Directly across from the body, someone had painted a black "8" tipped on its side. The symbol for infinity...and something else.

"Lola?" he said.

Lola raised her head to look at where

he'd pointed his light. "Well, I'll be.... I haven't seen that since—" Her voice trailed off as she stepped closer to the graffiti. She flicked a gloved finger at the sign, and sticky black paint came off onto the latex, making her index finger a matched set with Daniel's. "It's fresh, so it could be from our guy. What do you make of it, Junior? Motive?"

"Vengeance," he said, with a certainty that made Lola shoot him a questioning look. But there were no questions in his mind, despite Lola's constant admonition to "never assume" when it came to piecing together evidence. The infinity symbol was one that he was all too familiar with, as well as the sinking feeling that came with any sighting of it.

"It belongs to a street gang. The Latin Cobras," he said.

Lola drew her thick eyebrows together, her gaze locked on the symbol. Daniel heard the scuffing footfalls of Polly's Tyvek-covered shoes step up behind them. "Didn't they fall off the face of the earth?" Polly asked. "I thought they were crushed after that whole Sanchez thing that went down."

That whole Sanchez thing… Daniel shook his head, as if that stupid gesture could clear it of the memories.

"How do you know, Detective?" Polly asked.

"I know," he said carefully, "because I was a Cobra."

Chapter Three

Nearly twenty-four hours after his little trip to St. X University, Daniel smacked the Valencia file against his desk and leaned back in his chair, causing the springs to squeak mightily. Oscar Valencia. He'd been about the same age as Daniel and his identical twin brother, Patricio, but Daniel couldn't remember their ever knowing a Cobra named Valencia.

The fact was, Daniel hadn't been a Cobra for all that long. He and Patricio had been orphaned at age eight, separated from their older brother, Joe, and baby sister, Sabrina, and adopted by the Rodriguez family, all in the space of one very traumatic year he didn't like to dwell on. The whole transition from being "the Lopez twins" to "the Rodriguez twins-whose-birth-parents-were-murdered-isn't-it-horrible?" had left them with big emotions they'd been too young to name, much less deal with. So they'd turned away from the wonderful people who were trying to fold them into a new family and adopted a family of gangbanger "brothers" instead. Daniel had naively thought the Cobras, those powerful young men with their slicked-back hair and cocky struts, could help him find Joe. Patricio thought the Cobras could help him fight through the pain. Only Patricio had been correct.

Daniel had run errands for the older boys in the gang—generally transporting mysterious, tightly wrapped packets from one end of the city to another. Patricio had acted like one of the older boys from the get-go. And the first time Daniel saw his twin with a switchblade flashing in his hand, circling another boy until attacking with the full sound and fury of his deep, deep anger, was the last time Daniel had called himself a

Cobra. At age ten, Daniel had gotten out, and he'd spent the next decade of his life trying to convince Patricio to follow.

Patricio had been out for eleven years now—he'd left when he and Daniel were nineteen, and he hadn't looked back. And though Patricio had built himself a respectable life since then, the old anger was still there, simmering beneath a surface of calm and self-loathing. Every birthday the twins had was a milestone, a reason to celebrate because Patricio was still here.

Daniel scrubbed a hand across his eyes, which felt dry and gummy from hours of poring over the backload of cases he and Lola were assigned.

Correction, from hours of poring over the *case,* not cases. Something about the Valencia file was nagging at him, and he wouldn't stop worrying the various elements of the grisly murder until the pieces had started to slide into place. Valencia. Oscar Valencia…

In an almost subconscious movement, his hand shot out and grabbed the telephone receiver on his desk, and he used a slightly chewed Lou's Garage pencil to dial his brother's cell phone.

Patricio answered before Daniel had even heard the phone ring. "Yo, Danny Boy."

He had no idea why Patricio called him Danny Boy—it wasn't like they were the least bit Irish. But now was definitely not the time to discuss stupid nicknames. "You busy?"

Daniel heard Patricio chuckle softly on the other end of the line. "I'm always busy."

"Yeah?" Daniel leaned back once more in his chair and caused the hinges to shriek again in protest. "What is it today, Hollywood? Extreme skiing or freestyle rock climbing? Or maybe you decided to jump out of an airplane with nothing but a bedsheet and a roll of duct tape?"

"Fun-n-n-ny. You're a funny guy, bro," Patricio responded as snatches of several conversations taking place around him seeped through the phone. "Just having a drink with Mr. High-Maintenance and a woman he picked up from makeup. No big."

"Drinks?" Daniel sat up abruptly, causing the chair's back to smack him in the back half a second later. "Be careful there."

Patricio just sighed. "I'm having a Coke, *madre,* so chill. And how about telling me what you want? I have to get back to my esteemed employer. I'm off duty, but you know how he is."

Daniel felt a smile tugging at the corners of his mouth. Patricio ran a bodyguard service to the stars, one so successful, he didn't even need to advertise. Word-of-mouth brought him plenty of L.A.'s elite in need of safeguarding from stalkers, overeager fans or jealous rivals, and Patricio protected them better than a portable, bulletproof bubble—with a lot more discretion. He didn't talk to the press, didn't gossip with his friends, and didn't let his attention waver for a second.

At the moment, he was on a temporary assignment in Washington State, watching the back of one of Hollywood's most famous action stars. Jack Donohue had been Patricio's favorite movie hero, until he'd met the guy and found out Jack was afraid of everything—dogs, mean fan mail, the thought of the other actors in his film conspiring against him, spiders, heights, water and the occasional kitten. ("It had sharp little claws.") And, he had a thing about compulsively washing his hands that creeped Patricio out. Five months of working with the guy had finally culminated in Patricio dubbing him "Mr. High-Maintenance," quite possibly the only unprofessional thing he'd ever done since starting his business. Apparently, Jack Donohue out-diva-ed the hundreds of Hollywood divas Patricio had protected over the years.

But enough of that. If Daniel stayed at work any longer, he'd still be there at the start of his next shift. He took a slug of the lukewarm coffee sitting on his desk, then asked, "You ever hear of a guy named Oscar Valencia?"

"Nope."

"You sure? About our age, average height." Daniel took a deep breath. "He's somehow connected to the Cobras." Using the pencil to flip open the file, Daniel shuffled through the papers until he found a photo of Oscar Valencia taken before the fire, while he'd still been alive. "Had a shark tattoo on his left forearm." He squinted at the picture and brought it closer. "Weird."

"What?" Patricio asked.

"The shark is smoking a cigar. Shouldn't that be in its gills rather than its mouth? I mean, if you want to be anatomically correct and all."

He heard his brother's sharp intake of breath through the phone line.

"O.T. Mejia."

"O.T… Oh, my God." Pulling the photo closer to his face, Daniel studied the man's features. Comparing them to the Cobra's former first lieutenant, Daniel realized that if you took away the lines around Oscar's eyes and mouth, shaved off the mustache and wrapped a bandanna around his head in place of the conservatively short haircut, he was the spitting image of O.T.

In fact, he was O.T.

"He changed his name," Daniel said, and it was a statement, not a question.

"Yeah," Patricio responded. "After the Sanchez trial, I bet. Look, I have to—"

"I know. Back to Mr. High-Maintenance." It didn't surprise him that his brother didn't display even the mildest curiosity over why Daniel had brought up O.T. after all these years. Patricio didn't like to talk about that time. Ever.

The two brothers hung up simultaneously, leaving Daniel to mull over O.T.'s—or Oscar's—file.

He drummed his fingers on the desk, looking at the pieces in front of him. O.T.'s brutal murder. The infinity symbol. The fire. O.T.'s double identity. The killer knowing Celia's name. The infinity symbol. The fire.

That Sanchez thing.

And suddenly, it hit him with the force of a two-by-four to the chest, and he launched himself out of his chair, sending the papers inside O.T.'s file flying in all directions. They floated to the black-and-dingy-white tiled floor. Daniel ignored them and shuffled through another pile of folders on his desk, examining and then tossing them across the wood surface at a dizzying speed. And then he found what he was looking for.

With the address of a mysterious house fire that had occurred two weeks ago in hand, Danny tore out of the Robbery and Homicide Division station and got into his unmarked Crown Victoria, flipping on the siren and shooting the portable flashing red light onto the roof before he'd even put the car into Drive.

A few minutes and several traffic violations later, he pulled up before a house in East L.A., or what was left of it. Yellow crime-scene tape surrounded the few blackened foundation bricks and piles of thick gray ash that were left. A jagged portion of the front wall and a single rose bush remained standing, though the wall looked like it could come down at any minute. The rest was a story for the insurance companies. But Daniel wasn't interested in what had burned.

He flicked off the car lights, and the ruin

faded into the darkness. The fire department had ruled the fire that had destroyed the house arson after finding traces of accelerant in an area in the back. According to the officers who'd been on the scene, evidence pointed to a cut-and-dried case of gang rivalry. Though the family members who had survived denied any gang affiliation, the kids had juvie records a mile long and neighbors claimed they ran with the Spanish Kings. Normally, a case like that wouldn't have come near Danny's desk, but he'd known the family a long time ago. Truthfully, the file had been about to come off his desk, until now.

Taking a flashlight out of his glove compartment, he switched it on and walked around the yard, shining the beam onto any flat surface that wasn't covered with grass or garbage. Across the sidewalk, on a pile of wooden crates, up the trunk of a fairly young oak tree, on the beat-up car left behind in the driveway. The light on his car was still flashing, bathing everything in front of him in a soft, pulsing red glow.

A quick glance at his watch told him it was 10:45 a.m. In the distance, he could hear people shouting, the strains of mariachi music playing from a scratchy turntable, blaring television sets, slamming doors. The houses around him were small and cheaply built, so it seemed like you could eavesdrop on any conversation going on in the neighborhood without too much effort. The words "*la hada,*" gang slang for "police", echoed from more than one house as people warned one another that Daniel had arrived, and closed their windows and doors to him.

Soon, a bubble of quiet surrounded the ruined house, and Danny worked in silence, searching. After more than half an hour of poring over the site, he hadn't discovered anything beyond your ordinary, run-of-the-mill arson on his first sweep. But it had to be there—his instinct was screaming that there was more to this fire than he'd first thought. He ran the flashlight beam across the property once more. Sidewalk. Crates. Tree. Car.

Back to the crates… Back to the tree.

Something caught his eye, and he stepped closer to the skinny oak. Someone had taken care to heap a small pile of mulch around its trunk, but it didn't quite cover what he'd seen at the base. He crouched down, aiming his flashlight close to the ground.

Tell me I'm dreaming. Tell me I'm wrong. Daniel prayed silently that the pieces in his head weren't about to fit together the way he'd feared. He reached out and fingered a deep, curving slash carved in the bark of the trunk, the wood underneath shining bright yellow in the flashlight beam. Then, brushing aside some of the mulch, he uncovered a tear-drop shape, tipped on its side. And then another.

Dios mío.

Someone had carved the infinity symbol into the wood. The same person who had painted it above Oscar's burned body, who had called Celia by name and had knocked her unconscious.

Daniel swore sharply, scrambling to his feet. Like a child's puzzle, the pieces fell easily and irrevocably into place before he'd even reached the car, confirming his worst fears.

He had to get to Celia.

WHEN CELIA OPENED THE DOOR to her condo, she had to fight the urge to close it again once she saw who was standing there. Without speaking, she leaned against the door frame, effectively blocking Danny from entering her apartment instead of inviting him in—and fighting the urge to pelt him with holy water and garlic. Unfortunately, past experience reminded her that when Danny Rodriguez wanted to talk to you, he didn't give up. Ever.

He mimicked her folded-arm stance, also leaning against the door frame. The result was that he ended up way too close for her comfort, looking straight into her soul with those golden-colored eyes of his that had always made her crazy. In fact, if he took one step closer, she'd be face-first in that broad chest of his, with those solid arms around her, and… Celia caved a lot sooner than she'd intended, pushing herself backward and breaking the silent standoff between them. "They couldn't have sent another officer, huh?"

Danny tugged at the collar of his white dress shirt, and it was then that Celia realized he was wearing a suit, not the blue uniform of the LAPD she'd once found so handsome on him. "What, you're not a cop anymore? You went all stockbroker on me since last night?" But he'd been in a suit last night, too....

"I made detective," he said quickly. "So, I need to talk to you about Oscar. Do you—?"

"You did?" Without stopping to consider what she was saying, Celia gave in to the burst of joy and pride that overcame her. "A detective with the LAPD? Omigod, Danny, you've wanted that since we were kids. That's incredible. That's—" Celia cut herself off abruptly, annoyed that she'd suddenly time-warped back to 1993, the year before Danny Rodriguez had ceased to exist as far as she was concerned. "Great," she finished coolly, toning down the Laker Girl enthusiasm in her voice and carefully schooling her features into her best attempt at sophisticated aloofness. "What did you need from me?"

And then Danny Rodriguez, damn his whiskey-brown eyes, started laughing softly, and she knew exactly which gutter his thoughts had descended into at the mention of how she could fulfill his needs.

"You are a jerk of the lowest order, and I hate you. Please ooze your way out of my doorway and back to the slime-mobile you arrived in." With that oh-so-mature comment, also obviously circa 1993, she reached back for the heavy wooden door and started to swing it shut. What was it about the man that made her feel nineteen again?

"I'm sorry, Celia. Celia!" He jammed his foot into the increasingly small space between the door and the jamb, preventing her from shutting the door in his face with one shiny, size-eleven dress shoe. So she did the only thing she could think of to do—she stomped on it. When she took her foot away, a light, dusty sandal print marred the glossy black surface of Danny's shoe.

"Come on, Cel," he said in response, not in the least bit angry. "You weigh, like, ninety-eight pounds. That didn't hurt."

She stomped again, harder this time, trying not to show how flattered she was that he thought her size-eight figure weighed ninety-eight pounds.

"Still didn't hurt."

"*Por el amor de Dios,* would you go away?" A few stray black curls fell into her eyes, and she blew them back in a huff. She waved him away with both hands. "Go. Shoo. Flee."

"I have to talk to you. About Oscar."

Celia froze in mid-shoo. Her ridiculous behavior was probably hampering Danny's investigation, and that wasn't helping Oscar any. She lifted a hand to squeeze the bridge of her nose in an attempt to stave off a sudden headache. "I already told Officer McManus and Detective Ibarra everything," she said into her hand. "The last time I saw Oscar was around 8:00 p.m. when he went into the basement with his mop and bucket, and I never heard anything suspicious. It was just the…smell." She dropped her hand and looked back up at him. "Why would someone want to kill Oscar, Danny?"

Danny ignored her question, all business now. She might as well have been any old interview subject, rather than the ex-love-of-his-life. Then again, maybe she hadn't been an ex-love at all. The way he'd treated her, she was probably more of an ex-lukewarm-interest.

"Did you know Oscar Valencia used to be a Latin Cobra known as O.T. Mejia?" Mr. Bigshot Detective Man asked.

"Yeah, I knew." She savored the way Danny's eyebrows rose in sudden surprise. *Gotcha, Rodriguez.* "St. X has a rehabilitation program for ex-juvenile offenders. Oscar was only seventeen when the Sanchez murder happened, and he wasn't one of the Cobras charged with directly killing Sonia. My father used his influence to get Oscar a job here after the trial, and he's been here ever since." She examined her smooth oval fingernails for a second, lost in thought. "Jay Alvarez, Mateo Garcia, and Antonio Rincon are here, too. Antonio is a hall director in Aquinas Hall, Mateo cleans the chapel and is getting his Master's in education, and Jay teaches set design in the theater."

"They change their names?"

"Nope. Just Oscar."

"You need protection," Danny said abruptly.

Celia just laughed, with only a touch of bitterness. "From you? Like I need a proverbial hole in the head, Holmes."

"Holmes?" Danny questioned, but then immediately answered himself. "Ah, Sherlock. I get it. Ha."

Celia shrugged.

Then, Danny's expression grew even more serious, if that was possible. He reached out and touched her arm. She stared pointedly at his hand until he dropped it. "Johnny Menendez died in a house fire two weeks ago. Arson."

Celia felt her knees buckle ever so slightly at the mention of the former Cobra's name. Danny obviously thought he'd found a pattern, and she didn't like where he was going.

"Cel, Marco Sanchez was released from prison last month. He's coming for the nine involved in his sister's death. And since you're the daughter of the attorney who plea-bargained seven of them down to misdemeanor charges, I think he's coming for you, too."

Chapter Four

Marco Sanchez was out.

Dios mío.

Stunned silent, Celia could only step back, doing the unthinkable and allowing Danny Rodriguez into her apartment. She did double duty for the university as a hall director, which meant she got a free and surprisingly large apartment and a little extra cash. The downside was that said apartment was attached to Sayers Hall, an all-women's dorm, and she could hear some of those women entrusted to her care giggling around the words "Dr. Viramontes" and "hottie" as Danny shut the door.

Nice.

The entrance opened immediately into

her spacious living room, with its turn-of-the-century detailing and carved wood trim. Danny settled himself into the expensive wine-red couch she'd splurged on last year. Stretching one arm across the soft velvet back, he tilted his head in a subtle invitation for her to sit next to him.

She folded herself into her antique rocking chair opposite him instead, grateful for the coffee table that served as a barrier between them. Then, just as quickly, she mentally cursed herself for feeling out of place for a second in her own home. If anyone should feel awkward, it was Danny, while she should be basking in the comfort of her home turf.

But before she could indulge in even a little basking, thoughts of Marco Sanchez came flooding back.

A gangbanger with a rap sheet a mile long, Marco Sanchez had lived with his mother, brother, Paco, and baby sister, Sonia, in a tumble-down shotgun house in a rough part of East L.A. When her brother had refused to recommend her to the Insane Posse, the gang he ran with, for protection in the increasingly dangerous area, Sonia had turned to the Latin Cobras. Apparently, she had wanted in so badly, she'd jumped at the chance when the Cobra's first lieutenant, one O.T. Mejia, had allowed her to go through the initiation. Mejia had given her a choice: She could endure a "beating in," or being hit and punched by gang member after gang member until King Cobra Tone, the head of the Cobras, decided she'd endured enough. Or, she could choose a "seeing in," sleeping with all thirty-two male members of the gang.

Sonia had chosen a beating in. King Tone had never called "enough."

Sonia had died under the hands of at least eight Cobras, one of whom was determined to have delivered the killing blows with the business end of a broken glass bottle, even though weapons weren't normally part of an initiation.

King Tone and the boy with the bottle had been sentenced to twenty-five years without parole for Sonia's death. Celia's father, public defender Eduardo Viramontes, had presented a flawless defense for the remaining boys, managing to plea-bargain six down to lesser charges. He showed that the seventh, Danny's identical twin, Patricio, had not only had nothing to do with Sonia's murder, he'd tried to stop it, and Patricio had gone free.

Celia could still remember the rage that hummed through Sanchez's body as he'd stood up from his seat in the courtroom years ago, raising his arm to point directly at her father, the lawyer who had, in his mind, let the men who'd murdered his sister walk.

"I'll get you, old man," he'd shouted to Eduardo Viramontes, disbelief and a deep, deep anger in his black eyes. "I'll get your family. I'll get your friends. And I'll get every one of the punks you let walk today."

As the bailiffs had dragged him out of the courtroom, he'd still refused to stop. "You're dead! All of you! You're dead!"

Sanchez had been arrested for attempting to purchase assault weapons from an undercover officer mere weeks later. He'd gotten out and had been arrested again when he'd taken a perfectly legal shotgun and had tried to blow the head off of one of the nine Cobras he'd vowed to kill in court that day. Now he was finally out of prison.

And according to Daniel, he hadn't forgotten his promise.

She clutched her elbows, staring at a stray piece of thread lying on a corner of the multicolored, hand-woven carpet she'd picked up at Wasteland, an upscale secondhand store on Rodeo Drive. "You have to help them. Mateo, Antonio, Jay," she said to Danny, referring to the ex-Cobras who worked on the St. X campus. "They're good people—they've put the past behind them, like Patricio has. They don't deserve—" she paused, nearly unable to deal with the visions in her mind "—what happened to Oscar."

Danny rose abruptly and went to the bank of windows on the far wall, which had a view of the St. X soccer field, and a few high-rise apartments, which afforded glimpses between them of the pricey, pastel-colored houses dotting the Hollywood Hills. "Who's going to protect you?" He stared out through the glass, the expression on his face so placid, he might as well have been discussing the weather.

Are you afraid for me, Danny? Would it matter to you if something happened to me, if I were out of your life for good? The questions were on the tip of her tongue, ready to shoot out and fill the room with an uncomfortable silence. But then, at the very last second, Celia couldn't do it. She couldn't ask Danny whether it mattered to him that she was in danger or whether he was just doing his job. Because the thought of him actually answering her, with that detached manner and that too-calm look in his eyes, was more than she could take.

"I'll be fine." She unwrapped her arms and let them fall at her sides, forcing her shoulders to relax. "You know Papi's gone." Her throat tightened at the thought of her ever-cheerful father, who had passed away a few years earlier from a heart attack. Danny had come for the funeral. She'd barely acknowledged him, but she'd known deep down what a sacrifice it had been for him to be there for her. All those Viramontes family members, keening and crying around him. It's a wonder Danny's head hadn't exploded from the stress of witnessing all that naked emotion. "I don't think Marco's going to come after me instead," she said.

Danny turned toward her, his bow-shaped mouth flattened into a line. "I wouldn't be too sure about that, Cel," he said.

Reaching behind her, she pulled out an orange-and-gold Indian silk throw pillow and hugged it to her chest, her eyes dropping to study a knot in the hardwood floor by Danny's feet. She thought the movement had been subtle, but Danny moved away from the window and came to stand in front of her—once again way too close. He looked down at her from his formidable six-foot-four height. "You okay?"

She flicked her eyes upward, looking at him through her lashes. "Stop looming."

His dark eyebrows shot up in surprise. "I'm not looming."

"You so totally are," she countered.

"Am not. I—" He stopped abruptly and

scrubbed a hand across his face. "I'm not doing this. You win." He backed away and sat on the couch across from her once more.

When he was a safe distance away, Celia tucked her legs underneath her and began again. "Are you sure? That it was Marco who killed Oscar and burned Johnny Menendez's house? How do you know the two events are connected?"

Danny's eyes gazed past her shoulder, as if he could see his past projected on the cream-colored wall behind her. "We called Marco the Firestarter. Like the Stephen King novel. He had this gold lighter, and he liked to burn things with it—paper, table edges, the tails of the stray cats that lived in the area. It wasn't until I became a cop that I learned he liked to burn people, too."

Abruptly, his eyes snapped back into focus, and he leaned forward to stare at her intently. "Look," he said, "nothing's ever 'sure' when you're investigating a homicide, not until you have a mountain of evidence to prove it. But there's evidence connecting O.T.'s and Johnny's deaths, and my gut is screaming that we need to watch Sanchez. And every instinct I have says I need to keep you safe."

"You need, you need." She blew out a frustrated breath, still clutching the pillow, her fingernails making a soft whirring sound as they worked against the silk. "I can keep myself safe, and if not, I'll find someone else who can. The men who were involved are in more danger than I am. Leave me alone, Danny. Go warn them."

Danny rose and paced back toward the window, then returned, purpose and even a hint of anger apparent in the tension in his spine, the tight movements of his muscles. "Celia, your father never would have gotten involved in the Sanchez case if you hadn't asked him because of Patricio and me." He planted his hands on the back of the couch he'd been sitting on a few moments earlier, leaning forward and staring at her intently. She'd almost forgotten what it had been like to be the center of Danny's attention—he could look at you as if you were the only thing that existed in his world. It took her breath away—always had.

Celia shook her head, waited until her voice came back. "Papi was a public defender, consumed by the need to help keep poor Latinos out of prison. He would have found that case if it hadn't found him because you and I were…" What word completed that sentence? What phrase could accurately pinpoint everything he'd meant to her? "…acquainted," she finished, purposefully choosing a word that minimized it, minimized what they'd been together. "Will you go away now?"

"No." The word was spoken with a soft finality that chilled her almost as much as the news about Marco did. "We were more than acquainted, baby girl, and I'm going to keep you safe until whoever killed Oscar isn't a threat to you anymore. I owe you that much."

"You owe me some peace, Daniel Rodriguez," she said, choosing to pretend the words "baby girl" had never crossed his lips. Closing her eyes, Celia tapped her toes on the floor to start the rocking chair in motion, trying to project a calm she wasn't close to feeling. Though it was subtle, the anger that thrummed through Danny's body over the murders was the most emotion she'd remembered seeing from him in a long time. He'd never been big on compliments, had a hard time talking about his feelings in more than the vaguest generalities. And after Sonia Sanchez had died, he'd shut down completely, and their relationship hadn't been able to stand it.

Patricio had been a guilt-ridden wreck with a death wish after Sonia's murder and the trial, and Danny had devoted his energy to pulling his brother out of the darkness. All of his energy. He'd not only refused any help Celia had offered, refused to talk to her about what he was going through, and he'd pushed her away, again and again, until she'd finally left, quietly and without protest from either side. He'd tried to talk to her months later, tried to apologize, but by that time, it had simply been too late.

It had taken months, maybe years, for

Celia to get over Danny Rodriguez—made
all the more difficult by the fact that they'd
had a disturbing tendency to meet up peri-
odically over the years—but over him she
was. So he was making her feel off balance
now. So what? Get him out of her apartment, push him out of her space, and she
could go back to her regularly scheduled
life.

Eyes still closed, she smiled serenely as
she rocked back and forth in her chair. At
least, she hoped her expression was serene, revealing none of the echoes of long-
ing and heartache and betrayal from the
past that inevitably turned up whenever
Danny's life briefly intersected hers. "I
spent too long thinking of you, and I don't
think of you anymore. I like it that way."

She felt him move directly in front of
her. "You don't think of me at all?"

"Nope." *Serene, serene. You are serene, happy, completely unperturbed by
the fact that you are alone with your
emotionally unavailable jerk ex-boyfriend.*

"Not even a little bit?" he asked.

"Nope." She could smell his cologne. He still wore the same Armani scent he'd always worn, and it still made her crazy. She'd once said yes to a date with a man she wasn't even remotely interested in on an intellectual level, just because he'd smelled like Danny Rodriguez.

She sensed Danny lean over and plant his hands on the chair arms, a hairbreadth away from hers, and boy, was he looming now. "I still think of you," he whispered, his face too close, his breath on her cheek. "All the damn time."

Her eyes flew open, and it was all she could do to keep from kicking him. Since when had the man learned to talk like that? "You know what?" She knocked his hands away and leaned forward, still seated. "I don't care. I stopped caring after my five-hundred-and-fifty-seventh attempt to get you to open up to me, to let me help you and Patricio after the trial." She realized her hands were clenching around the chair arms in a death grip, so she took a deep breath and loosened her hold. But not before Danny had glanced down at her fingers, which undoubtedly revealed to him in all their white-knuckled glory that she did care. At least a little.

"You can't hate me forever, Cel," he said, kneeling down next to her chair so he could look her straight in the eye. He rested one hand next to hers on the armrest, so their fingers were almost touching.

She crossed her arms, tucking her hands under her elbows, and shot him a sideways glare. "I don't hate you," she said in a voice that was fairly dripping with calm. "Hate requires a lot more emotion than I'm willing to invest in you."

Danny ran his hand across his close-cropped black hair and sat back on his haunches. "Jeez, Celia, can I have a break here? I'm sorry. I've said that to you so many times, and you still won't forgive me."

"What's to forgive? You made a choice. Go, you." She pulled her gaze away from the windows just beyond his shoulder and back to Danny's face. And she wished, just once, that they could have had a conversation in the past eleven years that wasn't painful, that they could have one now. But she had no idea where to begin. She stood and laid a hand on his broad shoulder. Just touching him made her feel bittersweet.

"It's in the past, Danny," she said softly. "Let's just let it go."

He stood, briefly covering her hand with his before stepping away so they weren't touching anymore. Her hand felt cold, missing Danny's brief touch. And deep in her chest, her heart ached.

Not quite meeting her eyes, he nodded. "Fine."

He moved toward the door, all pent-up emotion and unfinished speeches, and then he turned on her, the quiet intensity in his eyes nearly knocking her over. "You go nowhere alone. Not until we catch San-chez or whoever murdered Oscar."

"Of course not," she said.

"I'll send McManus to watch your door tonight. You should probably get someone else to cover your shifts here, get away from these girls." His eyes flicked up and down the hallway, and a couple of peering faces ducked back into their dorm rooms.

"You send someone for Mateo, Antonio and Jay, too," she countered.

He nodded once, and then he disappeared behind the stairwell door.

And though she would have rather stuck a pencil in her eye than admit it to herself, Celia missed him once he'd gone.

EARLY THE NEXT MORNING, before the sun had even managed to break through the smog, Celia padded barefoot onto the blue-tiled deck of St. X's indoor, Olympic-size pool. As one of their perks, the faculty and staff all had keys to the gymnasium building, where they could work out after hours as long as they were willing to sign a waiver absolving St. X. and the phys ed department from liability if they accidentally drowned in the pool or dropped a weight on their own heads.

Under strict orders not to leave her alone until sunrise, Officer McManus had accompanied her, and now the cop was not-so-comfortably seated in the metal bleachers that lined the east and west walls, her formerly perfect French braid looking a little less than perfect, watching Celia prep for her workout.

Not that Celia usually exercised at 4:00 a.m.—she was *so* not a morning person. But Danny's words had stayed with her all night long, robbing her of sleep, and they'd eventually driven her out of her apartment and to the gym.

Marco Sanchez was released from prison....

OhGodohGodohGod.

Celia stared at the blue, unbroken water, not quite ready to jump in. She tugged at the shoulder strap of her electric-blue-and-green racing suit, apprehension making her feel as if she wanted to crawl out of her skin. She wondered whether Marco still had any of the banned assault weapons that he'd been arrested for purchasing. She wondered whether he'd use one on her.

Celia pulled her thin swim goggles over her eyes.

I'll get you, old man.

Overpowered by the impulse to run, to get away, to get out of the city, the state, even the country as fast as possible, Celia dove forward into the pool instead. The movement came more from a giant nervous twitch of her legs, rather than a calculated dive, and she ended up nearly belly-flopping into the water. She surfaced, coughing from the noseful of water she'd inhaled, and flailed to the edge, her arms stinging from where they'd smacked onto the surface.

As she clung to the pool's edge, still coughing and snorting, a pair of shiny black cop shoes moved into her line of vision.

"You okay?" McManus asked from above her, the corners of her pale blue eyes crinkling in amusement. "Because it looked like you suddenly got electrocuted or something."

"I'm fine," Celia said between coughs, covering her mouth with a dripping fist. "Just nerves."

"Hmm. Well, be careful," McManus said. "You can drown in an inch of water, you know. Maybe this many inches this early in the morning isn't such a good idea."

Celia got her breathing under control and, still clinging to the side, glared upward at the cop.

"I'm just saying." McManus blinked, shrugged, then walked purposefully back to the bleachers.

As if she didn't feel ridiculous enough, having police protection. Celia had tried to send McManus home when she'd first had the impulse to go swimming at oh-dark-hundred, but the woman refused to leave her side, saying her orders were to stay with Celia until sunrise. Damn Danny Rodriguez and his overprotectiveness, anyway. It just didn't make sense that Marco Sanchez would come after her, threat or no threat.

So not only had Danny made a very nice policewoman go without sleep all night, but he'd managed to embarrass Celia by first making her jumpy about Marco Sanchez, and second, made her swim like a spaz as a result of said jumpiness.

In fact, nearly every ill in her world could be blamed on Danny Rodriguez. It was quite handy—simplified things, really.

With one powerful thrust of her leg muscles, Celia pushed off the wall and moved gracefully into a side stroke, hoping to lose her worries—Danny's fault, naturally—in the cool water. The water enveloped her body, immediately driving away the last vestiges of exhaustion. But even after ten punishing laps, the apprehension, like Officer McManus, refused to go away. What if Sanchez hadn't been lying when he'd promised to destroy her father's life by destroying those around him? And, remembering Marco's black eyes when he'd delivered that threat, long, long ago, she wasn't too sure that her father's premature death would deter him from his goal.

I'll get your family. I'll get your friends.

After completing the tenth lap, Celia flipped over as she pushed off the side of the pool and settled into a rhythmic backstroke. The fluorescent lights twinkled above her as she swam. But even the familiar rhythm of exercise couldn't drive away the thoughts that had robbed her of sleep last night.

He's coming for the nine involved in his sister's death.

After her father had passed away, her mother had coped with her grief by moving to Honduras to be with their extended family for half of the year, which was where she was now. Celia had no brothers and sisters, so that left only her as the designated target from the Viramontes family.

It didn't make sense. She knew Daniel wasn't playing with her when he said he thought she was in danger, but she'd had nothing to do with Sonia's death whatsoever. Just because Marco had said he was going to get the Viramontes family all those years ago didn't mean he'd follow through.

Several meditative minutes later, Celia executed a final flip-turn at the edge of the pool when she'd done ten backstroke laps and segued into the breaststroke. As she bobbed through the water, she noticed the sky lightening above her, pale sunlight illuminating the edges of the tall, thin coconut trees that swayed outside the pool building. Time for poor Carrie McManus to go home and get some much-deserved sleep. Taking a deep breath, she did a surface dive, kicking her legs up in the air and submerging herself underwater. She propelled herself to the edge of the pool nearest where Officer McManus sat patiently in the bleachers, and then surfaced in a burst of bubbles, inhaling deeply as soon as her face cleared the water. Tugging off her goggles, she tossed them on the concrete.

Water ran down her face, obscuring her vision so she couldn't see the cop, much less make out anything but a vaguely bleacher-shaped blur. Scrubbing her eyes with one hand, Celia blinked until her vision adjusted back to normal.

McManus wasn't there.

"Officer McManus?" Celia called. There was no answer.

With one hand clutching the pale blue edge of the pool, Celia spun around in the water to check out the bleachers on the other side.

Nothing.

"Carrie?" she called.

A muffled thump sounded from the direction of the main exit.

Celia let go of the side of the pool and silently treaded water, waiting for another sound, for McManus to answer her, for someone to appear through the wide double doors.

Nothing.

The only sounds in the room were the hum of the lights above her and the soft ripples as she circled her arms and legs underwater. Well, maybe Officer McManus had had to leave and hadn't wanted to disturb Celia's workout. The poor woman was officially off duty, after all.

Sure, keep telling yourself that, Celia Inez.

Grabbing her goggles before kicking off the pool wall, Celia did a clumsy front crawl with her head above water, keeping an eye on her surroundings until she stopped next to a ladder. She climbed out and grabbed her towel, which lay nearby, and squished her way around the edge of the water to the women's locker room.

The vague sense of unease that had nagged at her since McManus had left subsided somewhat once Celia walked into the locker room. All she needed were a few seconds to make herself semi-presentable for the trip back to Sayers Hall, and she could grab her stuff and go.

The lockers were painted a cheery shade of mauve, complemented by flat, navy-blue speckled carpeting—both of which contrasted horribly with the red-and-white St. X Cardinals logo painted on the doors and the north wall. Obviously, the Phys Ed Department hadn't taken the school mascot into account when they'd chosen their decor.

Celia navigated the rows of lockers until she spotted hers. She spun the dial of her combination lock until it opened, then dragged her gym bag—a freebie duffel from when she'd opened her account with the Bank of Los Angeles—onto the wooden bench that stretched across the entire row. Stripping off her plastic swim cap, she dropped it onto the bench, where it landed with a small smack. Then she un-zipped the duffel's front pocket and fished around for her hairbrush when—

Bang!

Celia whirled around toward the noise, her brush falling to the floor with a muf-fled thud. The noise sounded like a locker door slamming, but after a few seconds of remaining completely still, Celia realized she should have been able to hear some-one setting down their bag, snapping on a nylon suit, padding toward the door.

Instead, there was only silence.

"Hello?"

Bang!

Celia's hands jerked up instinctively, as if for protection. Again, the sound, a little closer this time, was followed by utter quiet.

"Who's there?" she called again, her heart pounding against her rib cage in tri-ple time.

No one answered her.

With slow, quiet movements, she wrapped

the towel around her waist and tucked in the edges so it stayed there. Carefully, she pulled her flip-flops out of her duffel and dropped them in front of her feet.

Bang!

"Oh, God!" Celia flattened herself against her locker, knowing that this time, the sound came from the row on the other side of hers.

And then she got angry.

"That's it." Stuffing her hand inside her bag once more, Celia fished around until she found her keys with their pepper-spray key chain, courtesy of the St. X Women's Advocacy group, who had handed them out at their last Take Back the Night rally. She clicked off the safety device with her thumb. There was only one way out of the locker room, and she was getting out or she'd go down fighting.

Slinging her bag onto her shoulder, Celia slammed her locker door shut, creating a *bang* of her own. Hopefully, she wouldn't go down at all.

Deciding to abandon her flip-flops, which would no doubt live up to their name and make all kinds of noise as she made her way toward the exit, Celia started for the door, leading with her pepper spray. As she reached the end of her locker row, she took a deep breath and then peered around the corner.

Empty.

The aisle on the side of the room was also deserted, so, her heartbeat in her ears, Celia crept along toward the next row. She skimmed along the side of the lockers and then looked around them.

Also empty.

And so it went, until she was up to the last row before the exit back to the pool, which was only a few feet away from the fire door that led outside. Except for a large cooler that had been abandoned on the bench, the row was empty. So either the noisemaker had left the room and she hadn't noticed, or he'd be standing right on the other side.

Her chest heaved as she breathed, in and out, in and out, waiting for her nonexistent courage to resurrect itself and propel her forward.

Not a sound, not a movement. And then—

BANG! BANG! BangBangBangBang-Bang!

Celia screamed and shrank back as every locker door in the row beyond hers seemed to slam in succession with excessive force.

The last door slammed just around the corner from her, and she screamed again. Then, just as suddenly as it had begun, the noises stopped. Clenching her pepper spray tightly, Celia waited for a heartbeat.

Then another.

And another.

Silence.

What do I do now?

Conscious of every creak her joints made, every rattle her body caused as she moved away from the lockers, she crept sideways until she was on the end of her row. She ran her hands softly against the metal, moved slowly to peer around the corner and assess whether she had a clear path to the door or not.

Beneath her hands, the lockers shook

and rattled as if a weight had hit the top of them. She looked up.

Whatever it was, it was fast, and she only caught a shadow of movement when it ducked back to the other side. But her pursuer had dropped something before he'd hidden from her again, something orange and—

Cursing rapidly in Spanish, Celia raised her hands in the air and curved her body inward like a bow, trying to avoid the fiery object that fell to the very piece of ground on which she had been standing.

It floated lightly but rapidly to the ground. Though it was smoldering, it was small, not a threat to her, really. Then, her brain registered the image, and her body froze.

It was a photograph of her and her late father. And the edges were burning.

"I'm waiting for you, Celia," a voice whispered from behind the last row of lockers.

Chapter Five

Danny followed Lola into the medical examiner's office, a nondescript beige-colored building on the edge of East Los Angeles. They showed their badges and IDs to the guard behind the small Plexiglas window to the right of the entrance, and he obligingly pushed a button that opened the door in front of them. Lola pushed through and walked down a gray hallway, lit by what had to be the most annoyingly bright fluorescent lights in the state, made even brighter by the shiny, ugly Formica tiled floor.

They reached a door marked Autopsy and entered. The room was more of a closet, really, with cabinets lining one wall that were filled with powder-blue surgical scrubs, booties and masks. Lola and Daniel pulled the scrubs on over their clothes, though Lola had to abandon her beloved trench coat, and fastened the masks around the lower half of their faces. Then Daniel followed his partner through the far door to the main autopsy room.

Fluorescents blared down from the ceiling in this room, too, making every surface gleam in a way that was almost painful to the eyes. A long steel sink—a trough, really—lined one entire wall, the backsplash dotted with faucets. A plunger sat in the far corner—he didn't want to think about what kinds of stuff plugged Polly's drains. Not that he was squeamish, but he couldn't imagine the day-to-day details of taking apart bodies for a living. The opposite wall had a countertop running along it, on which lay various bottles, scalpels, scales, rulers and other sundries whose uses were probably best left remaining a mystery.

In between the sink and the cabinet, at the far end of the room, tiny Polly Singh stood behind a seven-foot steel gurney.

Dressed in blue scrubs and white latex gloves, Polly was bent over a body laid out on a cold, metal table, a yellow paper tag attached to its blackened toe. Her fall of glossy black hair half obscuring her face, she looked like a delicate porcelain doll from India that had suddenly decided to go serial killer.

But Polly hadn't killed the body laid out before her. She was just a little too fascinated with finding out the whys and wherefores and whos behind that death for most people to be comfortable around her. Grossed-out as most of the free world was by her career choice, Daniel liked Polly. Her black sense of humor amused him, and she was damn good at her job.

She raised her head when they walked in, and a completely unhinged grin crossed her tiny oval face. Daniel would have bet the last Corona in his fridge that she practiced that look in the mirror. All the better to freak out rookie detectives, my dear.

"Detectives Rodriguez and Ibarra! What a pleasant surprise. You're just in time."

Polly picked up a tool that resembled gardening shears and snapped the steel jaws open and shut. Apparently, it was time for Polly to open up the body and see what was inside. Nice.

Lola yawned. "Yeah, whatever. We heard you were working on Valencia today. You have anything for us, Dr. Singh?"

"Why, yes, Detective. Meet the man himself, right here." She waved her hand over the body on the gurney, like a demented game-show hostess. Daniel and Lola moved closer, and at his new angle, he could see that Polly had already done her Y-incision on the victim from shoulder to abdomen and had broken through the victim's rib cage. The shear-snapping had obviously been Polly's idea of a joke.

"You've already opened him up, huh?" Lola said. "Good."

Polly pretended to look astonished. Then again, with her obvious delight in the macabre, she might not have been pretending. "Good? You missed the best part. Why good?"

"That rib-crunching noise is nasty,

Singh, and you know it," Lola retorted. "Now, enough with the mental torture and tell us what you know."

The young woman put her rib-crunchers down, the crazy grin on her face fading into an expression of pure professionalism. He had to hand it to her—she might have a twisted sense of humor, but Polly Singh was the best M.E. on the coast, he'd stake his life on it.

"I positively identified the body as that of Oscar Valencia, aka. O.T. Mejia, based on the fingerprints I took at the scene. After examining his stomach contents and what you told me about his scheduled dinner break at work, I'd estimate the time of death at about 9:15-9:30 p.m. the night he was found." She moved her gloved hand as if to shove her hair behind one ear, then thought the better of it and just tossed her head to get it away from her face instead. "No trace under his fingernails or anywhere else under the body. Most of it probably burned away."

"Cause of death?" Lola asked.

"The fire. And I think you'll find this interesting." Polly pointed toward the victim's blackened face. "You see where the soot stains get darker around his nose and mouth?"

Daniel grunted an affirmative.

"It shows that he inhaled a lot of smoke at close range. Your guy was alive when he burned." She turned the victim's head to one side with her gloved hand. "X-ray showed a slight fracture on the mastoid process, a bone protrusion behind his left ear."

Before Daniel or Lola could do anything to stop her, Polly picked up a scalpel and made a lightning-quick incision along the victim's hairline. Then, inserting two fingers into the cut she'd made, she peeled back the scalp, showing them the hairline crack on the bare, eggshell-gray skull.

"You know," Daniel said, "we would have just taken your word for it."

"Yes, but it's more fun this way," she informed him matter-of-factly. "Anyway, it looks like the perp surprised him from behind with a blow to the head, and that's how he got the opportunity to set poor old Oscar ablaze."

Daniel shook his head. Poor guy. Not a nice way to go. "Any idea how he did that? The fire?"

Polly pointed at him with the index finger of both hands, as if she was miming two pistols. "I'm glad you asked," she chirped. Turning to grab a small metal tray that sat on a rolling table behind her, she showed them what she'd found. "I dug a few pieces of this out of his left leg just a few minutes ago." She pushed four small, shiny objects around the tray with one gloved finger. "Already sent some of the same I'd found earlier this morning to the lab."

Bending closer to get a good look, Daniel saw that the objects in question were thick chips of glass, colored a bright green. While Polly obligingly held the tray, he tipped each of them over, examining them from all sides. A couple of the pieces were warped, he noticed, with tiny bumps on one side. It only took him a second to figure out what those bumps might mean.

"Looks like they came from a beer or wine bottle," he said.

Lola raised an eyebrow. "Possibly."

Polly took small tweezers and pinched a small fragment of sooty gray fabric, blackened at the edges. "Now, I'm just a medical examiner, not a lab tech, but this looks like cotton to me. I had a few pieces of this couriered to the crime lab this morning, along with fragments of the vic's clothing—which were denim and flannel, by the way."

Lola peered at Polly over her Unabomber glasses. "Did the lab tell you anything yet?"

Polly clicked her tongue. "You know I'm not supposed to waste my time with that. I find the evidence. You guys interpret it."

Lola just kept on staring.

"All right. I bribed a friend who works there with a promise to bring him Starbucks for a week. The lab's on my way here, and I had a theory I wanted to check out." She put the fabric and tweezers back on the tray and set them on the shelves once more. "He ran it through the gas chromatograph to test for accelerants. Fabric, even when burned, is perfect for that kind of testing, because the accelerants get absorbed into the fibers."

"So, what did he find?" Daniel said. He didn't need the Gas Chromatography 101 lesson, but he didn't mind listening, either. Polly's sharp mind and insatiable curiosity had just saved them days of waiting for the results, so he'd wait for her to sing the entire soundtrack to *Oklahoma!* if she felt like it.

"Traces of gasoline and castile soap," Polly said.

Bottle glass, cotton fabric, soap and gasoline. It didn't take Daniel more than a second to figure out what recipe called for those ingredients—a recipe that had been a particular favorite of Marco's back in the day. "Molotov cocktail?"

Lola nodded in agreement. Molotov cocktails were usually the crudest of the homemade bombs, constructed by filling a wine bottle with gasoline, topping it off with a gasoline-soaked rag used as a fuse.

You lit the fuse, threw the bottle, and when it broke, it usually caused a nice little explosion. However, Molotov cocktails were notoriously hard to get right. You couldn't fill the bottle up too much, or not enough oxygen would get to the fuel to cause an explosion. Their guy had not only gotten the mix right—looking at poor Oscar—but he'd known enough to add liquid soap to the mix, which made the burning fuel stick to whatever it was thrown at, like napalm.

Polly shrugged. "Maybe. That's what I'd think if I were a big-heap Homicide Special detective. But I'm just the M.E."

No one else at the scene had found additional shards of glass—those were probably at the as-yet-to-be-discovered location where Oscar actually died, if their Molotov hunch was correct. Daniel made a mental note to see if the fire department arson investigators had discovered the cause of the Menendez fire. If that, too, had been a Molotov cocktail…

The shrill notes of Beyonce's "Naughty Girl" echoed in the austere room. Lola reached into her pocket and pulled out her cell phone, snapping it open and putting it to her ear. "Ibarra."

"'Naughty Girl'?" Daniel and Polly mouthed at each other. Daniel grinned—who knew Lola had a wild streak in her? His partner scowled at them and made a motion with her hand for them to be silent.

"Uh-huh." She turned and walked to the other side of the room, leaving Polly and Daniel alone with the body.

Polly winked at him, and the bug-eyed, unhinged grin was back. "Sure you don't wanna stay for the rest of the autopsy?"

"You're a sick woman, Polly," Daniel replied.

"Junior!" Lola snapped from behind him. God bless Lola and her impeccable timing. He turned away from Polly and the body.

"Dispatch just got a call from St. Xavier," Lola said grimly. "The gymnasium is on fire, and Celia Viramontes is nowhere to be found."

THE CHARRED SCENT OF THE burning photograph filled her nostrils, bringing memories of what happened to Oscar back in full Technicolor force. He'd been such a big man, so strong, and he'd still died. And now Oscar's killer was behind those lockers, calling her to come out and face him, and she…dammit, she was strong, too. Celia tore her eyes away from the photo and raised her pepper-spray canister in front of her.

She could hear Oscar's murderer—Marco?—breathing softly on the other side of the lockers. He was waiting for her to come around the corner, just as he'd said. Waiting for her to try for the door.

Which was precisely what she had to do, because it was the only way out. And Celia wasn't about to just sit there waiting, like some dumb starlet in a B-grade horror film. No, this pyromaniac was going to at least lose an arm or an eye before he took her out, that was for sure.

She glanced at the picture again, its edges black and curling. The only visible part of the photo that hadn't burned was Celia's wide, toothy grin, like a perverse version of the Cheshire cat from *Alice in*

Wonderland. Oscar had died by fire. The message of the photo seemed to be that she would, as well.

Like hell.

Grabbing a stray shoe off the ground, she patted the smoldering photo scrap until it was no longer burning. Then she checked out the sides of her row again, relieved that no one was coming around the corners, that he was still waiting. She could hear his soft breathing, slightly to the left of her behind the lockers. He'd expect her to come around the sides, and then he'd have her.

Her eyes flicked up toward the ceiling.

With a quick motion of her fingers, she loosened the towel around her waist, and the damp terry cloth puddled around her feet. Tucking her pepper-spray canister into the top of her suit, she slowly and quietly moved to stand on the wooden bench bolted to the floor. A large plastic cooler sat on one end, and Celia gingerly climbed on that as well, taking care to keep herself balanced in the center so it didn't slide out from under her. The cooler made her just about the right height to...

Leaping upward, Celia smacked the top of the lockers with her hands and pushed down while swinging her legs into a sideways split. Her legs cleared the top and she swung them around and in front of her torso, ending up in a seated position on the lockers, her feet dangling on the other side. Not ideal, but good enough. Without looking down to see where her tormentor was, she quickly scrambled into a standing position. Then, with one powerful push of her legs, she leaped once more into the air, grabbed a pipe hanging from the high ceiling, and swung her body gracefully toward the door, landing mere inches from it.

Heaven bless her high school gymnastics coach.

As she felt someone move behind her, Celia whipped her pepper spray out of her swimsuit and pressed her thumb against the top of the canister. Her arm swung out and back, so the stream of fluid flowed behind her. With a loud yell, she headed for the door.

Something crashed at her heels, with a

sound like breaking glass, but she kept running. As she pushed through the swinging door, she felt an intense heat at her back, small pinpricks of pain on her calves, but she didn't look to see what it was.

Still spraying and shouting, Celia ran past the pool, moved through the pool entrance into the hallway, and didn't stop until her bare feet skidded onto the dew-damp grass of the quad.

On the crisscrossing sidewalks before her, students ambled in groups of two or three toward the cafeteria or their classes. Celia released the pepper-spray button and clamped her mouth shut, all too aware of the stares she was getting from students and, oh, God, a smirking Dr. Chevalier from the French department. Behind her, Celia heard a bell clanging.

"Well, all right, Dr. Viramontes," a male student said as his group of three—jocks headed for an early-morning stint at the gym's weight room, judging by their running shorts and fingerless weightlifter's gloves—stopped to take in her dripping, disheveled appearance.

Didn't she used to have nightmares about being caught naked in the middle of campus? she thought as she caught her breath and her pulse started to slow. She glanced down at her blue-and-green bathing suit, with its stupidly high-cut legs and, the cool morning breeze on her skin reminded her, low-cut back. Being here wearing only her suit was cutting it close.

One of the young man's friends elbowed him sharply. "That's, like, sexual harassment. Of the librarian, you loser."

As the two started to bicker, a third young man in their group simply cleared his throat behind a closed fist, making a valiant attempt to keep his gaze locked on Celia's face. "Is everything okay, ma'am?"

"No, it's—" she began, but was interrupted by a familiar voice.

"Don't you miscreants hear that? There's a fire alarm going off in the gym." She turned to see Jay Alvarez, the set designer from the theater department and former Latin Cobra, approaching. "Now, back away from the gym doors before you hurt yourselves, and leave Dr. Viramontes alone."

The guys stared at the building in puzzlement. Finally realizing that the source of the clanging sound was the gym's interior **fire alarm,** Celia did as Jay had suggested **and backed** away from the doors. Craning her neck to look around the corner at the far side by the pool dome, she saw a wisp of black smoke was just starting to curl into the sky.

Celia wondered whether or not Carrie McManus was still inside.

A pair of fire trucks pulled into the parking lot on the far side of the gym building, sirens wailing, and as she turned to run toward them, to tell the firefighters about McManus, she felt someone lay something soft and dry across her shoulders. Jay had stripped off the lightweight denim shirt he'd been wearing over a white T-shirt and covered her with it.

"*Gracias,* Jay," she said, her mind just barely registering her colleague's thoughtfulness.

"What's going on?" he asked her in Spanish.

"Long story," she said, responding in kind. The three young men looked at them with blank faces and then moved on down the quad, closer to the fire trucks. "We'll talk later, I promise."

She made to start running toward the trucks, then stopped herself at the last minute. "Jay, would you stay here and watch the door? Keep the students out of the building? I think there's a cop inside who might need help."

At his answering nod, Celia pulled the lapels of the shirt closed with one hand, feeling damp patches forming in random spots from the water on her untoweled body, and took off running along the side of the building. Her bare feet slipped on the damp grass as she quickly made her way toward the firefighters. Small crowds of students heading towards the cafeteria for six-o'clock breakfast were gathering along the quad to watch the scene, and a group of firefighters jogged past her in their bulky black-and-yellow gear, waving students away who were standing too close to the building.

As she approached the edge of the parking lot, a beige Crown Victoria skidded to a stop next to one of the trucks, a flashing red light perched precariously on top of its roof. The doors swung open, and Danny and his partner got out simultaneously. Detective Ibarra jogged toward the center of the action, while Danny had eyes only for her.

As soon as they were close, he reached for her, as if he were about to cup her face with his hands. But then he glanced at the people around them and pulled back at the last minute, and she felt only the faintest touch as one of his fingers briefly skimmed her jaw.

"You're okay." It was a statement, not a question, and relief was written all over Danny's face before he schooled it into the detective-style professionalism she was getting used to seeing there. Everything but his eyes, which were still taking her in. He lifted a hand as if he were going to touch her arm, but of course he didn't, instead letting it hover mere inches from her body. And damn that body, it wanted him to touch her again, wanted the comfort.

Wanted him.

Before she could wrap her head around that troubling, to say the least, emotion, he turned away from her to observe the commotion around them—students trying to see what was going on, firefighters steering them away and wrestling with their equipment, red lights flashing on the two trucks parked nearby, sirens still screaming. He looked back at her once more, his body practically humming with the need to hurl himself into the center of the chaos.

"I'm okay. Go." He did touch her arm then, briefly, but as he turned to leave her, she clutched at the rough fabric of his dark gray suit jacket, cursing her stupidity at letting her mind become clouded by Danny's presence. "Danny, you have to find Officer McManus." As quickly as she could, Celia described McManus's sudden disappearance and the hostile person in the locker room who'd probably started the fire.

Something like fear flashed across Danny's angular features, but the emotion was gone as quickly as it came. "Stay put." His voice was soft, gentle even, but somehow he managed to put more authority into those two words than her most hard-core professors from grad school. Then he was running toward the building, tugging Detective Ibarra inside with him. And all Celia could do was wait, as smoke poured out of the gym's roof, not knowing whether Oscar's killer was still waiting inside.

"SIR, I CAN'T ALLOW YOU to go in there."

Daniel flashed his badge at the firefighter who tried to block their way, but the man didn't budge.

"It's too dangerous," the firefighter shouted over the alarm, which seemed twice as loud near the doorway as it had been in the parking lot. Even with half his face obscured by his bulky hat, Daniel would have put him in his early twenties. "You'll have to stay out here."

"One of my officers is inside," Daniel shouted back. "I have better information than you on where to find her, and we don't have much time. So either you let me in or you have a good cop's death on your conscience."

It only took a second for the firefighter to make a decision. "I'm coming with you."

Daniel led the way to the pool, having been to the gym as a guest when Celia had still been a student at the university. He hooked a right at the front desk, then moved down a short hallway that was filling up with smoke by the minute. He knew that a wide set of five or six stairs and a wheelchair ramp lay about fifteen feet in front of him, but the smoke obscured it almost completely. Coughing, he crouched low, just barely able to make out the white-painted rail bisecting the stairs.

"McManus!" Lola rasped, then dissolved into a series of hacking coughs herself. The alarm all but drowned out her words, and he doubted Carrie could hear them.

She's a good cop. God, don't let her die like this.

He looked around at the halls shooting off

in four directions around them. Before them, down the one most obscured by smoke, was the pool, where Celia had last seen McManus. It made sense that she'd be somewhere down that hall. But if he were wrong...

He didn't want to think about what would happen if he were wrong.

The air grew thicker around them, and the heat made Daniel want to shed his suit jacket and rip off his tie. But he kept moving, scanning the doors lining the hall for a clue, a hint, anything that would lead them to Officer McManus.

A figure, nothing more than a darker gray blur inside a cloud of smoke, darted out of a doorway.

Lola pulled her gun out of her shoulder holster and aimed it forward. Daniel shoved the firefighter who'd accompanied them against the wall, shielding the younger man with his body. His hand traveled to his own gun.

And then another firefighter materialized before them, supporting a woman wearing a pink smock with his arm. The woman, presumably a building janitor, still clutched a cleaning rag, into which she was coughing violently. Her dark hair was caught up in a hairnet, giving it a distinct spherical shape around her head.

Daniel backed away from the wall and their escort, the hand that had been about to pull his gun falling back to his side.

"The building janitor," the firefighter holding the woman shouted at them. "Said she heard someone down that hallway." He pointed a gloved hand at the narrow corridor to their left. Daniel nodded and took off running, leaving Lola and the first firefighter behind.

The first thing he noticed was how much thinner the smoke was the farther one got from the pool area. The second thing he noticed was the blue plastic chair propped against an office door, purposely wedged under the doorknob to keep it closed.

Daniel kicked the chair away and yanked open the door. Carrie McManus lay on the floor immediately inside, her skin pale and waxy except for an ugly black bruise blossoming on her temple.

THE WAIT WAS AGONIZING, and more than once, Celia was tempted to bolt past the firefighters guarding the gym entrance to find them herself. But then, finally, Danny and his partner reappeared, supporting a coughing, watery-eyed Carrie McManus between them. Danny gestured toward the ambulance that had recently arrived, and Ibarra steered McManus toward it. And then he headed back to Celia.

"Where was she?" Celia asked as he approached.

"Trapped in a supply closet," he responded.

"Oh, God, is she okay?" The bruise on McManus's temple was visible even several feet away, which couldn't be at all good. The firefighters seemed to be bringing the gym fire under control, but Celia shuddered to think of what could have happened to the cop, trapped inside as she had been.

"She'll be fine," Danny said tightly.

To anyone watching them, it would have

looked as if Danny were discussing the weather, he was so calm. But Celia knew better. The way he was standing so very still, his jaw clenched tightly around the words he spoke, told her volumes. Danny Rodriguez was about to lose it. Which for him meant he might glare at her or something crazy like that. But she still knew what that glare would mean.

"I'm curious about the timing," he said, his dark eyebrows drawing together into an almost-glare. Oh, yeah, Danny was about to go ballistic on her. She crossed her arms and waited.

"McManus said she went to investigate a noise over an hour ago and was attacked and pushed into the closet by someone unseen," he said calmly. "Dispatch sent us here fifteen minutes ago. If I give you ten or fifteen minutes to realize McManus was gone, that still means you were alone in that building with the whackjob who started this fire for half an hour." He looked away toward the gym for a second, blew out a frustrated breath, then focused his otherworldly gaze back on her. "What gives, Cel? Are you trying to get yourself killed?"

Celia narrowed her eyes. "Of course not. I was swimming."

His mouth flattened. "Do you mind telling me what you were thinking? You weren't just endangering yourself, but you put a good cop at risk, too. From now on, no more swimming."

Celia glared at him and opened and closed her mouth a few times, not able to speak for a few seconds, and then— "Okay, first of all," she said, jabbing her finger toward his chest. "Who says you can walk back into my life and start dictating what I can and cannot do? Second—" she jabbed again "—it was sunrise, which was when Officer McManus told me she was going home."

"Celia," Danny said calmly.

"Third," she continued, running over whatever it was he wanted to say, "I'm sorry. I feel awful enough about Officer McManus getting hurt, and I don't need you to rub my face in it."

He pushed her finger to the left, so she

was pointing at the orange trees by Donne Hall. "Celia, point that thing somewhere else. You're going to hurt somebody."

She shook her hand violently until he let go. "Fourth—" Jab. "—I didn't ask for protection. Or advice. Fifth…"

"Celia, will you calm down?" Danny was still displaying the calm and patience of a Zen master, while she felt not even an ounce of her usual equilibrium. Not to mention that without styling products, her curly hair was starting to dry, which meant she had about fifteen minutes before it began an uncanny impression of Diana Ross's hair, circa 1970. This was so unfair. Every time she ran into Danny in her mind's eye, she looked fabulous— perfect hair, perfect outfit, perfect skin. But more often than not, when her path really did cross his since they'd broken up, she looked like she'd recently been struck by lightning.

And then, just as quickly as her anger had hit, it started to fade. She wasn't really upset with Danny for dictating anything to her. All she knew was that when he was around, anger was the easiest thing to pull out of the complex whirlwind of emotions she was caught up in. "I just wish—" She couldn't even look at him.

"What is it, Celia?" He moved closer, so she could feel his warmth at her side, even though he wasn't touching her. "What do you wish?"

"I wish you'd just go," she said softly, still staring at a patch of grass in front of them. "I'll be okay. I just want you to go."

He exhaled, and they stood together in silence. She wondered if he, too, was thinking about the eleven years of heartache and arguments and awkward conversations between them. They hadn't seen each other much since their relationship had faded away, but when they had, it had been enough to keep the old wounds open, and Celia was always surprised by how much they still hurt. Just last week, she'd been convinced she was over him. But now her guilt over Carrie being hurt was accompanied by something else, something all too familiar....

Danny finally broke the silence. "I'm

worried about you, Cel." When she stole a glance at him, she saw he'd bowed his head and was staring at the same patch of ground she'd found so fascinating moments before. Then he looked up once more, turning his otherworldly gaze back on her. "I always worry about you."

The effect of his words was like dropping a wet asbestos blanket on a campfire, and the last few embers of her temper died as quickly as they had flared, giving way to a hollow ache in her chest. "Don't," she said thickly, turning away.

She nearly smacked right into Detective Ibarra, who had apparently witnessed the entire exchange from beside them.

"Is there a problem here, Junior?" the woman asked, peering at Danny through her smeary, thick-lensed glasses.

Still looking at Celia, Danny crossed his arms. "No problem, Lola." He leaned back against the hood of the car they'd arrived in. "I have a favor to ask you."

Ibarra raised a silver eyebrow over her glasses but remained silent, waiting for Danny to go on.

Her intuition practically screaming, Celia could only watch him and wait. She didn't quite know where he was going yet, but she had a strong feeling she wasn't going to like it.

"Celia's an old friend, and she's in danger," he explained to Ibarra. "After what happened here today, I don't trust anyone else to protect her."

Okay, now she knew, and she *really* didn't like it. Not one bit. "Excuse me?"

"That sucks, Rodriguez," Ibarra replied, ignoring her. "They're going to stick me with Landau as a temporary partner, you know. The man never talks. It's eerie."

"Sorry, Lola," Danny said.

"For 24-7?" Lola asked. Danny nodded in response to the abbreviated question.

Ibarra sighed, shoving her hands deep into the pockets of her voluminous trench coat, which covered what was actually a very nice aubergine suit. "So you'll take leave?"

His tongue touching the chip on the end of his front teeth, Danny nodded again.

"That doesn't mean...?" Celia began. "You can't really think...?"

Oh, *hell* no.

Chapter Six

"You know, I'd rather set myself on fire than have you trailing me everywhere." Celia, freshly showered after her ordeal at the pool and dressed for her evening shift in wide-leg black pants and an acid-green, Mandarin-collared shirt, pushed angrily through the glass library doors. She'd twisted her hair up and secured it to the top of her head with two black-and-gold chopsticks, but a few curls had sproinged loose and bounced as she walked. Daniel, who'd changed into jeans and a gray Lakers T-shirt he'd had in the trunk of his car, followed behind.

"I'm so not letting you into my apartment," she continued without looking back at him, which gave him a pretty nice view, all things considered. "So you'd better get that whole 24-7 business out of your head right now."

"We'll see," he replied calmly. He didn't care if he had to hang upside down in front of her bedroom window—he was going to stick to her like a fungus until the man who was threatening her was caught. But he didn't think it would come to acrobatics— he'd wear her down. Always did. "And come on, Cel. Aren't I a better alternative to self-immolation?"

Celia smacked through the half door to the library's front desk, and it swung back hard, nearly taking out his knees. Daniel caught it with one hand and gently pushed it out of his way as he walked through.

"You know, the jury's still out on that one," Celia replied, her back to him as she shuffled through a stack of books on the desk.

"Drama queen," he said, feeling a smile tug at the corners of his mouth. Calling Celia a drama queen was sort of like calling the ocean wet, or his brother Joe's dog ugly.

She bent down to grab something in a floor-level cabinet, so her response of "Overbearing, stubborn man" came out muffled, though hardly out of his earshot.

You'd think after eleven years, Celia would be over being angry at him, but apparently not. Figuring silence was better than continuing their sixth-grade-level discussion, Daniel reached over and picked the top book off her stack. He backed away and sat down on a nearby padded stool, opening the book and skimming the dust-jacket blurb.

"Give that back," she said.

"Just looking." He kept on skimming.

He heard her sigh in exasperation. "You wouldn't like it."

He raised his eyes to look at her, his head still bent toward the book.

"It's a mind-numbingly pedestrian account of first contact with an alien race. Trust me, nothing to scream about." She turned to her desktop computer and tapped at the keys, then picked up a stubby pencil and scrawled something on a piece of scratch paper. "Have you read David Weber?"

He grunted a negative.

"I read my way through his Honor Harrington series a while back. It's this great space opera—a cross between *Horatio Hornblower, Star Wars* and *Xena: Warrior Princess.* Right up your alley, since you seem to have such parochial reading tastes."

He smacked the book he was holding shut and slowly smiled at her. This was more consideration than she'd showed him in a long time. "You remember my reading tastes?"

She slid past him and glided into the stacks, her silk pants fluttering around her amazing legs as she walked. He tossed the book aside and followed.

"I remember way too much about you, Holmes." She tapped a peach fingernail on the spines of several books shelved at her eye level. "Space opera, cyberpunk and futuristic dystopias all the way. Not a classic to be had on your nightstand." There was an awkward pause as the two of them contemplated the last time Celia had seen his nightstand. He cleared his throat, and she scrutinized the shelves with amazing intensity.

"Aha. Here it is." Celia pulled the book out from where it was sandwiched between several others by the same author and handed it to him, the faintest pink still staining her cheeks. "Now, go." She shooed him away with one hand. "Read, and stay out of trouble."

He bit his bottom lip and grinned at her. "What if I get bored?"

Celia dropped her hand and tilted her head at him, looking genuinely perplexed at the thought of getting bored. That was pure Celia all the way—she was always running at Mach 2 with her hair on fire, and she wouldn't know how to be bored if she tried.

He stepped into her space, lowering his eyelids to half mast. Such a bad idea, but he always seemed to lose his mind whenever Cel was around, which had been less and less often over the years. Now she was here, and he was stunned that he still felt...way too much. And some perverse impulse inside him made him want to mess with her world as much as she was messing with his.

To her credit, she tilted her chin upward to keep his gaze and didn't back down when he stepped closer. "That stairwell in the back looked pretty private," he murmured, laughing softly. "We could go inside and..." His gaze dropped to her full lips, slathered in a pink-tinted lip balm that smelled like cherries.

The loose ends of her hair bounced as she reeled back in shock, but then she quickly assumed a blasé expression, hooded eyes, wry mouth and all. "Daniel, my tastes—in men and in pastimes—are a lot more civilized today than they were a decade ago."

"What about a year and a half ago?" he asked, unable to stop himself.

"A year—" She cut herself off, looked down at the floor. Now her expression just looked sad. "A very big mistake," she said softly. She raised her face to look at him, and he couldn't speak, couldn't think of anything to say to her that would take away that sadness, that would make her trust him again.

"Why do we do this to each other?"

He just shook his head.

Dropping her gaze to somewhere over his left shoulder, she lightly touched the fingertips of one hand to his chest, gently pushing him out of her path. "Excuse me. I need to get to work."

As she moved quickly through the stacks and into her office, he could still feel the five points on his chest where she'd touched him. Oh, man, this was so not good. He'd meant to mess with her, and she'd blown his mind instead. He should have known it would happen, because that's what always happened whenever they'd met over the past eleven years.

She closed the door behind her, but the front wall of her office was made of glass, affording her the ability to watch over her domain but very little privacy. Daniel folded himself into a study carrel that boasted a perfect view of her desk if you tilted it at a slight angle, which he did. He opened his book, watching her over the top of the cover.

After a few seconds of fidgeting behind her desk, obviously feeling him staring at her, she looked up, glared at him, and spun her desk chair around so all he could see was its padded gray back.

Why can't you just let it go, Chief?

Why, why, why. That had always been the question when it came to Celia and him. They'd started dating in high school, ended their relationship when they were nineteen—she was in her junior year at USC, and he was a patrol cop for the LAPD. It should have been easy to forget a woman he'd dated at such a young age. It should have been easy to move on, find a nice blonde or a redhead with a sweet temperament and a squishy right hook. But it wasn't. Their relationship had officially ended eleven years ago, but he and Celia had made each other pay for that fact a thousand times over since then.

The last time he'd seen her, a year and five months ago, Rita Henderson had dragged him to the Arthur Murray dance studio in Century City for ballroom dance classes—very much against his will. Rita, a woman he'd casually dated a few times, had been blond, with the requisite sweet temperament and squishy right hook, not to mention a disturbing thing for unicorns. But that day had been her birthday, and he'd been unable to disappoint her by refusing her request.

So he'd agreed to go, not knowing that in the middle of the Arthur Murray Studio B dance floor, wearing a flowy red dress that hugged her full hips and small waist perfectly, Celia was waiting.

She was also with another guy.

She saw Rita and him as soon as they entered the room. Raising her eyebrows in a casual hello, Cel immediately turned her back on them and tangoed the other guy to the opposite side of the room—leading all the way, despite the instructor's frequent call-outs of "Ms. Viramontes, let your partner lead." So even though seeing her was like a punch to the stomach, he took Rita into his arms and picked up on the basics of the tango in no time. He was Mexican and Honduran—dancing was not an issue.

After the first hour, the instructor called out that they were all to switch partners. Rita twirled away on the arm of a guy Danny could have sworn he'd recently seen in a deodorant commercial. Bodies swirled around him, pairing up without giving him so much as a glance. And before he knew it, he and Celia were in the center of the room. Face-to-face.

She looked around, a hint of desperation in her face before she realized they were it—the left-overs who would be forced to pair up. Then she rolled her eyes and held out her slim, brown hands, their nails tipped in red to match her dress. "Fine. Whatever. Let's just be adults about this."

He pulled her into his arms.

Once again, he'd been trying to play mind games with her, but as was usually the case when it came to Celia, things didn't work out according to plan. The feel of her in his arms—again, finally—took his breath away. So when he didn't say or do anything, Celia aimed their clasped hands outward and tried to steer him across the room.

Her actions brought him back, and he immediately retaliated by flexing the arm around the small of her back, pulling her tightly against his chest. Her cherry-red mouth dropped open in surprise as she stumbled against him, and the strength left her arms. Looking straight into her warm brown eyes, he began to lead, and, miracle of miracles, she started to follow.

The instructor, who'd been calling directions to her students, fell silent. Slowly, as they danced, the other couples broke apart and stepped back, two by two, against the studio walls and mirrors. Then it was just the two of them.

"Who is she?" Celia finally gasped her first real words to him as he dipped her over his arm, running a hand across her collarbone.

He pulled her back upright, twirling her on his outstretched arms across the floor while he simply advanced. The hem of her red dress flared around her show-stopping legs. "Date," he said simply when she'd stopped twirling, because that's all he could manage.

"Serious?" Brushing a hand against his chest, she promenaded around him, her back strong and her brown eyes flashing.

"Nah. We've gone out a couple of times. What about him?" Danny cocked his head toward Celia's date, who stood forlornly against the wall in his light blue, button-down oxford and khakis. "Get you to join the Young Republicans for Tax Reform yet?"

He twirled her so her back was against his front, raising their right arms over their heads, and then skimming his hand down the side of her body. He looked down at her face, and her eyes fluttered shut briefly. "Brad is a fun guy," she murmured.

He spun her to face him and advanced on her as she retreated. "Right. Fun. Looks like a real animal."

"I don't date 'animals.'" She turned her head to the side in time with the music, kicked her leg out, and then she was advancing, and he was backing away. "Anymore. And it's not like Betty Crocker Barbie over there looks like she's rocking your world." Celia glanced over at where Rita was standing, and Danny followed suit, noting that she seemed to be enjoying her conversation with the deodorant guy. "Is she actually wearing a Peter Pan collar?" Celia asked.

She wrapped one leg around his, and they swiveled their bodies together the way they'd just learned, "for drama," as the teacher had said. He clicked his tongue at her and gave her a slow smile, amusement washing over him as he realized that Celia was jealous. She'd never made disparaging comments about people she didn't know unless she had a good reason. "Not nice, Cel."

"Sorry," she said, mid-swivel. "It's a cute Peter Pan collar. She's very cute."

"Thank you," he replied, twirling her away from him.

"Whatever." She twirled back in, and they moved smoothly across the room once more.

The music rose to a crescendo, and Celia kicked her leg up, her skirt flaring out, and then her heel was resting on his shoulder. The other students gasped at her flexibility—thank heaven for gymnastics—as he put his hand on her ankle, moving back and taking her with him. They moved seamlessly into a low lift and he spun her around, put her back down, dipped her once more. The music ended, and he was bent over her, his mouth so close to hers, he could feel her breath on his face. The other students started clapping.

"You're beautiful," he murmured under the sound of the applause, before he could stop himself.

She jerked back, nearly causing him to drop her. With one arm still around her waist, he helped her straighten, and she pulled out of his arms. "You have a date," she muttered through her teeth, practically spitting out the final *T* as she smiled at the other students.

"I think she's more into that actor guy she's talking to." When Celia turned to look at Rita, still batting her long eyelashes at her dance partner, he moved closer to her. "Stay with me tonight," he whispered in her ear.

"*I* have a date, you cad," Celia whispered back. The instructor asked the students to join him and Celia on the floor, and soon they were surrounded by other couples. Rita and the actor seemed to want to stay together, but Brad was making his way toward them with purposeful strides.

"You know how good we are together." His mouth moved against her flushed cheek as the music started. He didn't want to let her go. Not without a promise.

"At dancing. Just at dancing." Her shoulders rose and fell with her deep, almost gasping breaths, and her hands were clenching his shoulders as if she were drowning.

He laughed softly in her ear. "More than just dancing, baby girl."

He felt Celia's fingertips dance lightly on the back of his neck, where his hair touched his collar. "I—" she began.

Someone loudly cleared his throat next to them. "May I cut in?" Brad asked primly.

"I'll be waiting," Danny said as she slipped out of his arms.

And later, after he and Rita had amicably decided that that night's date would be their last, after he'd gone home to his La Brea apartment, after he'd turned out the lights and paced, restless, in the dark for longer than he cared to remember, she came.

As he'd known she would.

They'd spent one very hot night together, and then, by morning, the ghost of Sonia Sanchez rose to tear them apart once more.

Celia had started talking about it again, and he hadn't known what to say. He'd hurt her when he hadn't opened up to her after Patricio got out of the Cobras. Truth was, he just…couldn't. Everything, every big emotion, especially the negative ones, was something to hide, something to swallow. Straighten up, put a smile on your face and push it all away, pretend everything was just fine. It was how he'd dealt with the deaths of his parents, with losing his brother, Joe, his baby sister, Sabrina. So when Patricio had gone through his darkest moments, Daniel had shut down and shut Celia out, focusing only on his twin brother, on keeping him alive. And when the worst was all over and he'd tried to get Celia back into his life, she didn't want any part of him. The woman was the queen of holding grudges, damn her Viramontes pride. And he couldn't find the right words to tell her how sorry he was.

So they did this figurative dance every time they saw each other—they met, were blown away by the still-potent attraction between them, acted on it more often than not, and then, she'd bring up that time with Patricio after Sonia's murder. She always made it clear that she wanted something from him, but for the life of him, he didn't know how to give it to her. He'd apologize, but then she'd always ask him if he'd do things the same way if he could do them all over again.

And he always said he would. He couldn't see doing anything differently. Patricio had needed him, so he'd been there. And he couldn't see how getting all weepy about it with Celia would have helped their relationship. Fact was, he couldn't have if he'd wanted to. It just wasn't the way he was built.

He'd told her that, again, the morning after their meeting at the dance studio, and she'd left him. Again. He'd sworn, at that moment, to get her out of his head once and for all. It had almost been working, until he'd found out that her life was in danger. He'd keep her safe, or die trying. And he wasn't ready to die just yet.

He also knew he'd have her before this was all over—he could see it in her eyes every time she looked at him. They were repeating the same pattern, locked in the same steps they'd danced a year and a half ago. They'd have each other, and then she'd leave, just the way she always left.

Resting his forehead on one hand, Daniel peered through his fingers at Celia, who was staring blankly at her desktop, lost in her own thoughts.

They were a mess, the two of them.

When he'd realized that she was in danger, he knew he had to help her. Because worrying about her only made everything worse, and he knew he wouldn't have a moment's peace unless he was right by her side to keep her out of harm's way until it was all over. And then, maybe after all was said and done, he could finally walk away. Maybe by forcing himself to be beside her day in and day out, they could work through some of the crap they'd put each other through and find peace. And then, he could do what she kept asking him to do—just go, just leave her alone for good.

Sure. You keep telling yourself that, Chief.

Celia's door swung open and she barreled out, her face pale and her hands shaking.

"Danny!" she called, her voice tinged with hysteria. He didn't even have to think. Within seconds, he was right by her side.

"I just got a call from Jay Alvarez," she said. One of the ex-Cobras involved in the Sanchez murder, who now worked in the St. X theater, he remembered.

"He sounded like...." Her voice trailed off. "Danny, he sounded terrified."

Chapter Seven

Celia couldn't shake the cold that had enveloped her at the sound of Jay's voice. There was an almost unreal, unbelievable quality to the knowledge that she herself was in danger, but it seemed all too real when the danger involved friends and colleagues.

The first thing Jay had said when she'd picked up her phone was to ask her not to say a word. Then he'd immediately told her he had something important he wanted to discuss with her. He'd asked her to meet him in the theater, backstage behind the newly built set for the upcoming production of *Once Upon a Mattress*, in ten minutes.

And then, without even letting her say goodbye, he'd ended the conversation.

But what had disturbed her most was the weird whirring noise she'd heard in the background, the sharp click just before he'd hung up. And the odd tone in Jay's voice, as if he had rehearsed his words. Oh, the fear behind those words sounded real, but something about the measured cadence of them hadn't fit.

Her mother had always told her to trust her intuition, and her intuition was screaming its head off right now.

As she'd jogged across campus as quickly as she could in her stack-heeled Mary Janes, she'd given Danny the quick-and-dirty version of the conversation. She was tempted to keep her misgivings about the situation quiet, telling herself that she was being ridiculous. But then, knowing that there were students in the theater at that time of day whose lives could be at stake, she told him that her instinct was screaming danger.

Without questioning her, he immediately whipped his cell phone out of his inside jacket pocket and called Detective Ibarra, asking her to meet them at the Sally M. Wainwright Theater, the tallest building on campus due to the five-story-high fly space above the stage.

As they approached the building's glass double doors, Danny looked as if he wasn't sure about letting her go inside. But when she told him that there were students in the building, he went inside, and she followed.

They moved together into the grand lobby. Before them was the ticket office, with two staircases lined with bronze banisters flanking it on either side, leading up to the main theater. To their right, posters for *Once Upon a Mattress,* as well as several of the theater's past productions, decorated the brightly lit wall. To their left was the entrance to the small, intimate recital hall, as well as a hallway leading to the theater faculty offices, various classrooms and the main stage. Celia motioned for Danny to follow her as she took off down that hallway.

She could hear the sounds of a lecture

coming from the recital hall, which were soon drowned out by the sawing and hammering of the crew putting the final touches on *Mattress*'s sets in time for opening night that weekend. She led Danny past the set builders—glancing at them to ensure that Jay wasn't among them—past the green room, and into the side-stage area.

Several students dressed in Renaissance-era finery filed past them, including a couple of the young women who lived in Sayers Hall.

"Hey, Dr. Viramontes!" Darcy Larkin chirped happily, shoving the veil hanging from her green, cone-shaped hat back behind her shoulder.

"Hi, Darcy. Tanya." Celia pulled herself up sharply, forcing herself to smile and relax, even though she was ready to jump out of her skin. Something about Jay's voice had just been…wrong. "Just get out of rehearsal?"

Tanya Sorenson reached behind her and undid the top button at the neck of her heavy-looking gold-brocade-and-purple-velvet gown, her blond curls falling into her round face as she did so. "Yeah. We're taking a dinner break, and then we're back at it again. You know Phil." She stopped fussing with her gown and pointed to where the show's director stood several feet away, shouting and gesticulating wildly at a boy with a paintbrush in his hand. "Total slave driver."

"You coming to the show?" Darcy asked.

"Wouldn't miss it," Celia replied. Truthfully, she'd been looking forward to the lighthearted musical, and it would be even more fun with Darcy and Tanya to mentally cheer on.

Both girls turned a curious eye on Danny. Tanya opened her mouth and seemed about to ask Celia who he was, but Celia cut her off. "Have you seen Mr. Alvarez around? Detective Rodriguez and I have a meeting with him."

Darcy and Tanya looked at each other, raising their eyebrows and pursing their mouths. "*Detective* Rorguez," they said in stereo, as if they'd just made a momentous discovery. Grinning, they turned back to Celia.

"Not since yesterday morning," Darcy said, finally pulling the cone hat off her sleek red hair.

"Scene and Light Design 101," Tanya explained. "She's failing."

Darcy elbowed her. "Am not!"

"Darcy, your drama disintegrated into tiny little pieces when Jay picked it up." Tanya made fluttering motions with her hands. "Come on!"

Darcy shook her head and rolled her cat-green eyes. "Jay wouldn't fail me just because the glue I used sucked. He loves me. Well, Dr. V., we're off to get some dinner. Want anything?"

Celia told them no, thanks, and the girls left, chattering at each other as they worked at the buttons of their dresses while walking.

"Jay, huh?" Danny said. "He's on a first-name basis with the students?"

Celia smiled as they stepped onto the stage. Phil Markus, artist-in-residence and the show's director, had finally stopped yelling and stomped past them in a huff, the object of his tirade slouching sadly along behind him.

"Yeah, Jay's like that," she said. "They adore him."

Hearing a rattle above them, they looked up to see a heavy curtain crashing down toward them at a frightening speed.

Danny grabbed her arm and pulled her out of the way. As the metal bar attached to the curtain's bottom edge clattered to the ground, Celia knew that it could have done some damage had it hit her.

"Sorry, Dr. V.!" a voice called from the wings, presumably where the curtain levers were.

"It's okay," she called back, willing her pulse to slow to its normal speed again as she and Danny walked along the outer edge of the stage. The scrim—the semitransparent curtain that had just been lowered—was designed to give the set behind it a two-dimensional look to members in the audience. But even through that veil, she could see that the set was stunning—Jay and his team had outdone themselves.

The front of the stage, around the orchestra pit, had been transformed into a stack of books, with fairy-tale titles embossed on the spines she could see from above them. The top of the stage was an open book, and sitting above it was a quaint, intimate medieval village that looked as if it had come straight out of a Disney cartoon. Tiny cottages with thatched roofs and windowboxes stuffed to the brim with bright flowers lined the upstage area, along with a couple of "Ye Olde Shoppes" with pottery and baskets on display. They'd even added a small well with a bucket on a rope and pulley, which sat in the corner, stage left. Papier-mâché trees with silk leaves towered behind the set, giving it a cozy, enclosed feel, which was further enhanced by the giant mural painted on the backdrop, featuring a brightly colored castle and its flowering garden.

It almost made her forget why they were there.

She and Danny walked around the scrim and onto the set itself, which was even more stunning in full, three-dimensional color. Celia could hear the last of the students trickling out for their dinner break, and finally, they were enveloped in near-complete silence. Even the set crew seemed to have taken off.

"Jay?" she called.

When the set designer didn't answer, Danny walked to the backdrop, Celia close behind, and followed it stage left until he reached the end. They looped around the edge and walked back around the other side, into the dimness of the backstage area. A flexible desk lamp illuminated a long table before them, which was taped off like a grid. Various props lay in the grid squares, labeled with names written on pieces of masking tape. Danny reached out and briefly fingered a veil on a crescent-shaped velvet hat that was marked as belonging to "Winifred."

They walked past the prop table, their footsteps echoing on the black-painted wood. The area beyond the table was dusty and bare, save for a couple of stray pieces of wood and an abandoned screwdriver.

Above them, something creaked.

Danny's head snapped up.

"Jay?" Celia called again. Craning her

neck, she squinted upward, into the inky blackness of the unlit fly space. When there was no response, she turned to Danny. "There are catwalks in that space. Maybe he's up there fixing something."

"Maybe I should go up," he said. "See if I can find him and get this over with."

Thinking about the relative flimsiness of the catwalks suspended five stories above their heads, her intuition was screaming again. Or maybe that was just pure cowardice. "He'll be here," she responded, mentally noting that they were both speaking in near whispers, even though there was no one to hear them and no show going on around them. She looked up toward the ceiling again, able to just make out the outline of the steel-mesh walkways crisscrossing the ceiling.

Something creaked again.

She could see the faintest shadow, darker black on black, swell slightly on one of the catwalks.

"I'm going up," Danny said. "Where's the door?"

Celia's eyes flicked involuntarily to a

lone door on the far wall, half hidden because it was painted black like the walls and floor. Danny noticed the movement and turned to investigate.

"Are you sure that's such a good idea, Holmes?" she asked, preventing herself at the last minute from reaching for him. Instead, she squinted into the darkness above them once more, but couldn't make out anything that looked remotely human.

"Why? You said yourself there are a lot of people hanging out here during the day." He twisted the knob and swung the door open, revealing a narrow stairwell and an elevator. "We need to find this guy, so I'm finding him. I doubt if he can hear us way up there."

True. But she still didn't want Danny going up there. At least not alone. She stepped through the door behind him. He immediately turned around, nearly knocking into her in the narrow room.

"Cel, why don't you stay here? You hate heights."

She didn't know what to say to that. *Because I'm worried. Because I can't shake*

*this feeling that you shouldn't go up there.
Because I think something terrible has
happened to Jay in the ten minutes since
we spoke, and even though I'm not much
protection, I don't want you to go up there
alone. Because I still feel way too much for
you, and we need to finish this once and
for all, and we can't do that if you get
yourself killed.*

"I just... Let's wait," she said lamely.

He reached out and fingered a stray curl
near her temple, and this time, she let him,
her fear getting the best of her.

"Why don't you go hang out by the set
crew?" he suggested. "If Alvarez shows
up, yell." Then he paused and looked at
her, really looked. He was standing in her
space, breathing her air, and she wanted to
cling to him and never let him go. Yes, she
was afraid of heights, but the thought of
Danny up on the catwalks alone with some
mysterious shadow she knew in her heart
of hearts wasn't Jay terrified her.

"I think it's dangerous," she said finally.

"I'll come back down in five minutes,"
he murmured. "I promise."

Her heart constricted. What if he didn't keep that promise? What if he couldn't?

SHE LOOKED AT HIM FOR a long time, then batted his hand away from her hair in a move that was pure Celia and walked off. He wasn't sure what he'd done to upset her this time, but he figured she'd feel better once they'd found Jay and were safely talking to the man in his office. He pressed the button for the elevator.

The up arrow light came on, but then it blinked off as soon as he took his finger away from the button. He tried again, but the up arrow light wouldn't stay on, and the elevator wouldn't come down. Jay probably had it holding at the top. Blowing out a frustrated breath, Daniel started up the stairway.

Several flights later, so many he'd lost count, he made it up the last few steps to another steel door. Good thing he ran every morning, or he'd have been toast. The door swung open silently on well-oiled hinges, and Daniel stepped out onto the catwalk.

The steel rattled ever so slightly at his

weight. He left the door open, and started to move along the metal walkway. "Mr. Alvarez?" he called. There was no answer.

But someone was up here with him. Daniel could hear him breathing.

Above and around him, more catwalks crisscrossed the fly space. As he moved forward, he could see where another walkway crossed his own, branching off into inky blackness.

"Jay," he called, "I'm a friend of Celia's. We'd like to talk to you."

He glanced down, through the mesh under his feet. The stage floor looked impossibly tiny, and even though he wasn't generally afraid of heights, his stomach still lurched in time with the slight swaying of the catwalk at the sight. The dark hardwood floor below was dimly illuminated by the stage manager's backstage lighting, but none of that reached up where he was. He could barely see two feet in front of him, the only light coming from a small window in the stairwell. He couldn't see Celia below.

Tearing his eyes off the faraway ground,

he slowly approached the far wall, and he could just make out a small set of stairs, which, when he followed them with his eyes, appeared to go up to another set of catwalks above him.

Suddenly, the walkway shook violently. Someone landed hard behind him, having obviously jumped from the second level of catwalks above. The stressed metal screamed in protest. Daniel spun around, his hand moving toward the gun tucked in a holster at the small of his back.

Unfortunately, he never got to it. He heard air rushing in his ears, and then there was a bright light as his forehead burst with a searing pain. Daniel's body whirled around, putting the attacker behind him, and he stumbled to his knees, gripping the thick metal wires that flanked him on either side.

Before he could move, the attacker swung again, air whistling as the long, thin piece of metal he was holding came down with vicious force. Daniel pivoted and raised his arm to block it, taking the brunt of the hit on his forearm. He hissed in pain, his arm dropping useless to his side as his fingers went numb.

With a roar, he tucked his shoulder and rolled—a gamble considering how dizzy he felt from the blow to his head and how little side protection those catwalks had. Fortunately, he'd calculated perfectly, coming to his feet a couple of yards away from the shadow behind him, still on the catwalk instead of floating in the air. He turned.

The shadow advanced, causing the walkway to tremble.

Gripping the wire that acted as a guard-rail with his working hand, Daniel waited until the attacker was close enough and then swung his leg in a powerful round-house kick. His foot caught the attacker in the stomach, and the man expelled a breath, his body arching back and slamming against the thin railing with considerable force. The catwalk, which had been vibrating slightly the entire time, shook alarmingly from side to side, the thick wires that held it suspended from the ceiling creaking.

The man fell to a crouch, causing the catwalk to lurch again. Daniel swore under his breath, almost missing the metal bar as the attacker swung it at Daniel's ankles. Just in time, he jumped out of the way.

He heard footsteps running up the stairs.

Dammit, Celia. He knew, beyond a shadow of a doubt, that she was the one approaching.

She'd told him there was only one way up and down, which meant that the man who'd just attacked him was standing between Daniel and Celia. Which meant that she could get hurt if he tried to escape...or if she came toward them.

He wasn't about to let that happen.

"Danny!" Celia stood silhouetted in the doorway, illuminated by the last rays of daylight that filtered through the small window behind her. She held a stubby two-by-four in her hands.

With a growl, Danny lunged at the man who'd attacked him. He aimed a punch at the man's jaw, but the man turned at the last minute, and Danny connected with his upstretched arm. The metal bar dropped to the catwalk with a clatter, then slid over the edge to fall end over end until it crashed onto the floor below.

"Cel, get back!"

She was coming at them like a shrieking banshee, holding the two-by-four like a club. For a brief fraction of a second, he admired her guts, then cursed her carelessness.

Taking advantage of Daniel's momentary distraction, the man pushed past him—away from Celia, thank God—and moved into the shadows by the far wall. Breathing hard, Celia stopped short behind Daniel, who'd made himself as large as possible to block her path and keep her from going any farther. He was torn between going after the man and keeping Celia and her stupid club as far away from the attacker as he could.

It turned out that neither choice would have made much of a difference. They heard a creak, and then a groaning sound, as if one of the metal walkways was bearing too much weight, and then…

At first, Daniel thought the man had taken a suicidal plunge downward, but then he realized it was a second body, falling to the ground without uttering a sound. The man himself had pulled on a harness and was lifting his leg over the wires that flanked the catwalks.

And then the man, too, was falling, except the fly wires strapped to the harness kept his descent slow and steady.

Chapter Eight

Before Danny could break around Celia to make for the stairwell, the dark figure five stories below them had unfastened the harness and was running across the stage, leaping into the auditorium.

Celia watched him go, and then, despite her fervent wish not to see what was below her, her eyes traveled to where a tiny figure lay splayed out on the floor like a rag doll. It blended in chameleon-like with the black-painted floor, making it hard to make it out at first, especially from her great height, but then... *Oh, no*.

"That was the stupidest thing I've ever seen you do," Danny hissed. Even in the darkness, she could see the scowl on his face, and it stunned her. Daniel had never been the scowling type.

She reached out, put a hand gently on his arm to soothe him. "Down there," she said softly. "We have to go to him." She knew, she *knew,* that the figure five stories below them, lying broken behind the beautiful set he'd created, was Jay Alvarez. And the knowledge broke her heart.

Danny didn't pursue his newly discovered ability to emote any further, even though she could feel his frustration with her, coupled with the fact that he hadn't stopped the killer, humming through his body. He moved back to the stairwell and ran down, obviously hoping he could still catch the man who'd been on the catwalks. Celia followed behind, moving more slowly, afraid of what she knew she'd find once she reached the bottom.

When she finally reached the ground floor, Danny had returned, batting aside the velvet curtain blocking off the side stage with more force than necessary. By the black look on his normally calm features, she knew the man had escaped.

Taking a deep breath, she stepped out of the doorway toward him, trying not to look. But then her head turned, and the entire expanse of the backstage area came into view. The first thing she noticed was the hand—black, clawlike, and stretching out as if reaching for her. And, the *smell*... Celia covered her mouth with her hand, trying to block it out. But unfortunately, she couldn't black out the vision as easily.

Another pair of work boots. Another poor, tortured body. And this time, a blackened tool belt to let them know that this...raw, painful-looking thing had actually been Jay Alvarez at one time.

"Oh, no...." Celia started forward, wanting to go to him, but Danny had reached her by then, and he curved his arms around her to hold her back.

"Don't, Cel."

"Danny—" She struggled against his chest. It was too late, she knew it, but still she didn't want Jay to lie there all alone.

"It's a crime scene," he said, pulling her to his chest, rubbing his warm hands across her back until she stopped fighting and sank into his embrace. She felt tired, suddenly, more exhausted than she'd ever felt in her life.

She hadn't even known she was crying until her damp cheek came in contact with his T-shirt, leaving a small wet spot. *Marco Sanchez, how could you do this thing? How could you be so cruel in the name of your sister?*

Clenching her teeth, Celia swallowed, unable to speak for a moment. But something was wrong here, something beyond the mere horror of Jay's murder, and she had to put her grief away for a moment and address it. This must be how Danny felt, always compartmentalizing his emotions, tucking them away, out of thought and memory until he felt ready to take one out and deal with it. No wonder he'd made detective, with an ability to detach like that. She only wished it worked as well for her. But, as always, she felt too much, couldn't detach if her life depended on it. *The students loved Jay. It isn't fair.*

A cold, tight ball forming inside her chest, Celia pulled out of Danny's arms and pointed to where the body lay. Her skin prickled again as she thought of Jay burning, screaming in pain, alone with his killer and afraid. He was a good person. He'd deserved better than that. "There's something…" She paused, collected herself once more. "There's something inside his shirt pocket. Something shiny. It's out of place. It doesn't look burnt."

Marco Sanchez, how could you do this thing? She could kill him herself, easily, if he'd been standing here before her.

Daniel cupped her face with both of his strong hands, turning her gently away from Jay to face him. "Celia, look at me."

Her breathing hitched, and an angry sob escaped her lips, but she focused on Daniel, gripping his arms and holding on tight as the blackest of emotions swirled inside her head.

His gold-colored eyes met her own, forming a connection that was old and familiar and so very needed right now. "I'm sorry about Jay," he said. "I'm so sorry."

She closed her eyes, concentrated on the feel of Danny's hands against her skin, offering comfort, keeping her grounded. "He had a family," she said brokenly, trying not to think of Jay's wife, his small son.

She felt Danny's mouth brush hers, and instead of the white-hot electricity that act would have normally sparked, it made her feel comforted, when she'd thought nothing could comfort her.

"I'll find him," Danny murmured. "And he will pay for this, I promise."

"I know." Danny held her tightly, and she let him. They stood like that for several minutes, but then, the thought that they weren't getting any closer to Jay's killer made her pull away. "What can I do?"

He took her hand and tucked his cell phone inside it. "This will connect you to Detective Ibarra when you hit Send. I met her in the parking lot, and she started driving around, looking for Sanchez. Tell her to get back here if she hasn't found anything."

She nodded and made the call. Ibarra told Celia she hadn't seen anything suspicious, and neither had the people she'd interviewed who'd been standing outside the theater. When Celia informed him of that, Danny nodded and pulled a pair of latex gloves out of his pocket, tugging them on his large, tanned hands. She clicked his phone shut and watched in silence as he approached the body, bent down to gently pull a silver mini tape recorder out from under a flaking piece of Jay's clothing.

How could this happen, when Jay had only called her mere minutes before?

Danny hit the play button. After a small click, a familiar voice said, "Celia? Please don't say anything in response. Just nod your head and act as if you're having a normal conversation. This is Jay Alvarez, at the theater…"

Dios mío, it was the same thing Jay had said to her when he'd had her on the phone. The clicking noise. The static.

"I think we need to talk," the voice said.

"He had a tape recorder," she told Danny. "He recorded Jay's voice." No wonder her colleague had sounded like he was reading from a cue card. He probably had been, and who knows how long ago that had been?

She looked at the black, deformed shape, lying in the shadows before them, its skin alternating between angry, blistered red and flaking black patches. *Oh, Jay.*

Then Danny stooped down and picked up a piece of paper that lay with just a corner pinned under the body. He easily tugged it free, then straightened. It had her name written on the folded side.

Danny straightened up and unfolded the paper to read the writing inside. Even from several feet away, Celia could see the single word printed on it:

Soon.

DANIEL SPENT A FITFUL NIGHT on Celia's couch, unable to sleep, thinking every small noise was Marco Sanchez, coming for his girl.

Soon.

No, he would watch, and he would wait, and when that bastard made his move, Daniel would be ready for him. Because there was no way in hell he'd let Sanchez get to Celia, burn her like he'd burnt the others. He'd die first.

Once Celia got out of bed, he shadowed her every move, going everywhere with her except the bath. And even then, he told her to be out in five minutes or he was coming in. To his disappointment, she'd complied.

He also made several phone calls to the university president, asking her to send the students home until the LAPD cracked the case. She'd readily agreed but warned that it would take at least two days to finalize travel or temporary living arrangements for all 1,200 students, not to mention the hall directors who lived on campus.

He was just getting ready to follow Celia to her evening shift at the library—which was closed to students, though her work remained, she told him—when Lola showed up at Sayers Hall. Celia invited her inside the apartment, then disappeared into the kitchen.

"Look, Junior," Lola rasped without preamble, her husky voice the hallmark of too many cigarettes smoked "back in the day." She'd since quit, although sometimes when she was really wound up, he caught her sucking on a plastic surrogate that delivered a nicotine hit without blackening her lungs. "The body from the theater was Alvarez, and the lab discovered the same glass bits and accelerant trace that we got from Oscar Valencia. I'm sure you're not surprised, but we've officially got a serial on our hands." She whipped the plastic cigarette out of her trench coat pocket and inhaled deeply, still standing just inside the doorway, though Celia had asked her to make herself comfortable.

"And the Menendez fire?" he asked, knowing that Lola would have finished what he'd started regarding the fire before taking his leave of absence.

Lola wove the surrogate cigarette through the fingers of one hand, flipping it from end to end. "You were right on the money with that. The fire department says their evidence indicates that a Molotov thrown at the back of the house started the fire. Johnny was the only one home, at the time, so the perp probably had some inside knowledge. I told Landau and Peterson to interview the surviving family. See who had contact with Johnny in the days before his death and might have known his schedule."

Daniel leaned back, until he was half sitting on the back of Celia's couch. "So what about the evidence? I assume they found glass at the Menendez site—any of it a match?"

"Yeah, we got glass," she continued. "None of it's a match. The lab says the glass the chemicals used to color the bottle glass in all three cases indicates that the perp probably used vintage-wine bottles, all from different manufacturers. And there wasn't anything special about the cotton, just like Polly predicted."

Daniel mentally filed away the information for later, even though he wasn't officially on the case. Vintage-wine bottles—that could be helpful.

"I need you to come with me." Lola took another drag on her plastic cigarette. "Landau's driving me nuts, so I told him to go hover around the lab and nag them about analyzing the cigarette and footprint we found at the Valencia scene."

"They'll love that," he said dryly.

She grunted, hitching her small shoulders upward in a very odd little shrug.

"I can't leave Celia." He was dying to hear more about how the case was progressing, soaking in the small details Lola had given him from the lab report like a man suffering from thirst, but he wasn't about to leave Celia with someone else. That hadn't worked out so well last time with McManus. The thought of her alone, in the gym or in the theater if he hadn't been there made him want to lose his mind.

Lola raised a bushy gray eyebrow at him, and he briefly wondered if she somehow knew in which direction his thoughts had headed. "I brought you three big, brawny cops to keep an eye on her, and I'm leaving a couple more to watch over Antonio Rincon and Mateo Garcia."

Rincon and Garcia were the last two former Cobras working on the St. X campus, and if the pattern held, they were next in their killer's macabre lineup. As long as he could prevent Sanchez from getting to Celia.

Daniel didn't like leaving Celia, but he had to admit, the cops Lola had brought were three of the best—and biggest. Celia herself wasn't too happy about having a big, burly entourage for her shift at the library, but with the fact that it was closed to students, Daniel reminded her, there wouldn't be too many other people coming in to check out books, anyway. After a lot of back and forth and some unmanly pleading on Daniel's part, Celia finally relented, leaving him and Lola to make their way out to their trusty Crown Vic.

"So, about your theory that Marco Sanchez is behind this," Lola said from the passenger seat as Daniel backed out of the Sayers Hall parking lot.

"Yeah?" He put the car into drive and moved down the main access road, through the university's stone-and-iron main gate, and onto St. Xavier Boulevard, which would run into Wilshire after a few blocks. "Where are we going, by the way?"

"East L.A.," Lola said. "Marengo Street, a coupla blocks down from the East L.A. Occupational Center. By the little quickie mart on the corner that sells those melt-in-your-mouth tamales."

"Ah." He knew those tamales. Lola had introduced him a while back, and he'd been pleased to make their acquaintance.

She took another hit on her fake cigarette, her breath whistling through the plastic. "We have no hard evidence at this point tying Marco Sanchez to the crime scenes that we are aware of."

"We've got plenty of circumstantial evidence," he countered calmly, keeping his eyes on the road. "A motive plus a past threat to do violence. Not to mention the interesting timing of his being sprung from San Quentin just before the murders started."

Lola jabbed her cigarette in the air as if scoring him a point. "Yes, and the fact that you've been able to predict his future victims with unfailing accuracy is strong evidence indeed. It's enough that I was able to put out an All Points Bulletin for Sanchez's arrest, though no one has even caught a glimpse of him as of yet." Tucking the plastic cigarette into the inside breast pocket of her trench coat, Lola continued. "The fact that this is now considered a serial case helped me to bump Valencia up on Polly Singh's priority list. When I visited her this morning, she told me that Alvarez, like Valencia, was killed at another location. Menendez just happened to die in the fire at his home—no transporting the victim in that case, but Sanchez may have been warming up." She cleared her throat and shifted in her seat. "Uh, pardon the pun."

He smirked in response. Sometimes, Lola's twisted sense of humor rivaled even Polly Singh's. "So if we find the location where Alvarez and Valencia were killed, we'll probably find all sorts of concrete ties to our killer," he surmised. Spotting the sign he'd been looking for, Daniel followed the arrows until he pulled onto the on-ramp for Interstate 5 and merged into traffic.

"A veritable smorgasbord of evidence,

Junior. At least, I hope he's been too dumb to clean up after himself. But we may have a harder time finding it unless we find Marco first." Lola stared out the window at the houses and low-slung buildings lining the highway. "So far, we've got nothing from his contacts, and no one has seen him at his preprison hangouts. We've questioned his mother a couple of times, but she's not talking. Thought it might help if you came with me to see her this time."

She tapped the window as they passed a familiar red-and-white fast-food restaurant. "Ah, I could go for In-N-Out Burger right now. Love their fries." She turned back to face him. "Maybe we'll get lucky and we'll catch him sneaking out the back of her house. But if not, she might crack eventually and tell us where he is."

"Why not take Landau?"

She shrugged. "He's boring. Plus, he doesn't look exactly like Patricio Rodriguez, one of our suspect's possible intended victims. Thought that handsome face of yours might get some interesting reactions." He heard the rustle of her voluminous coat as she searched her pockets for something, followed by a faint whistle when she took another drag on her cigarette.

"I love it when you use me as bait, Lola." He gave her a wry grin while keeping his eyes on the road.

They took the same exit they would if they'd been paying Polly Singh a visit, and a few twists and turns later, they pulled up in front of a small but neat brick house on Marengo. Thick-leaved banana plants flanked the freshly painted white front door, and gardenias and flowering succulents spilled out of large terra-cotta pots on the steps leading up to a side entrance. Lace curtains covered the windows inside, and a blue Dodge pickup sat under the carport beside the house. He could hear Los Lonely Boys playing on the radio inside.

"Okay, Lola, let's do this." Danny and Lola got out of the car and approached the side entrance, knocking lightly on the screen door. The main door was propped open, and they could see glimpses of kitchen appliances through the screen.

"Paco!" a female voice called from inside the house. *"Abre la puerta!"*

Abruptly, the music cut off. Footsteps thumped through the house toward the door, and then a muscle-bound man of medium height, wearing a pair of cutoffs and a white wifebeater with a sleeveless flannel shirt over it, appeared behind the screen. "Yeah? What you want?" he asked gruffly. It wasn't Marco, Daniel knew, which meant it had to be his younger brother, Francisco Sanchez, aka Paco, owner of a boxing gym located conveniently close to the area hospital.

"Detectives Ibarra and Rodriguez with the LAPD," Lola said as they both flashed their badges. "We'd like to speak to Mrs. Sanchez."

"Is this about Marco?" Francisco said, still blocking the entrance with his formidable body. "Look, he didn't do nothing, man. He just got out of jail a coupla weeks ago."

"¿Quien es, mi hijo?" a low-pitched yet clearly female voice called from one of the back rooms. "Who is it, my son?"

"*La hada,*" Francisco growled, sneering as he said the Spanish slang for "the police," as if the phrase was profane.

"We just want a few minutes of her time," Lola said soothingly, switching to Spanish. Francisco stared at them for a moment, then finally grunted and stepped back.

Behind him, a tall, thick-limbed but pretty woman, probably in her fifties, stepped into sight. She was wearing a yellow long-sleeved shirt tied at the waist of her white capri jeans. A yellow flowered scarf was wrapped headband-style in her dark brown hair, which flipped up at the ends. "Francisco, let the officers inside, *muchachito,*" she said in a husky, deeply accented voice. She twisted a dish towel in her hands as they opened the screen door and stepped into her kitchen.

The room was small but clean, the walls painted a sunny yellow to match the patterned linoleum. White eyelet curtains flanked the small window over the kitchen sink, and several blue-and-green wine bottles lined the windowsill, filled with water and colorful flowers. Daniel made a mental note to ask about them. They were all markedly different, meaning none of them were likely to be a match to the Molotovs that had killed the three victims. But their presence was the kind of circumstantial evidence that would assist in making the case against Marco airtight.

"I'm Maribel Sanchez. Please." She gestured for them to sit in one of the plastic, yellow-flowered chairs surrounding her round, Formica-topped table. "Can I get you anything? Water? Juice? Coca-Cola?" The brand name was almost musical when spoken in her Mexican accent, the *C*'s hard and crisp.

"No, thank you, ma'am," Danny replied. He waited until Maribel Sanchez and Lola had seated themselves, then sat down as well, the chair legs squeaking against the linoleum when he pulled it back from the table. "Nice wine bottles. Antiques?"

Maribel looked at her improvised vases and smiled. "Oh, no. We drink the wine and if it comes in a pretty bottle, I can't bear to throw it out. And sometimes I find them at flea markets, or my sons bring me some they find."

"Mind if we take them with us?" Lola asked as she sat down, her trench coat billowing around her legs.

Maribel looked puzzled. "*¿Por que?* They are just old bottles. Some of them have—how you say?—sentimental value? Maybe if you had *un* warrant."

Lola flipped open a small notebook she'd carried in with her and jotted down a few notes. Maribel watched her for a moment, her forehead wrinkling with worry, then turned to Daniel.

"Did I say something bad?"

"No," he said reassuringly. "Not at all. Of course you can keep your bottles." *For now.* "Have any gone missing in the past few days?"

She shook her head. "No, they are all there." Maribel folded her arms on the tabletop and smiled, revealing a chipped front tooth. She was nervous—Daniel could see it in the way she clenched one hand tightly around the opposite wrist—

but she was obviously doing her best to hide it and be polite.

"When was the last time you saw your son Marco?" Lola raised her eyes from her notebook.

Maribel's eyes flicked up and to the right, where a calendar hung on the wall just behind Lola. "Oh, right when he got out of prison. We picked him up and brought him home for dinner. He stayed the night in his old room, but I haven't seen him since he left the next morning."

"Know where he went?" Lola asked, once more writing down notes.

Mrs. Sanchez shook her head. "He didn't say. He's not in trouble again, is he? He promised…" Tugging at the loose tied ends of her scarf, which hung over one shoulder, she squinted at Daniel. "You know, you look very familiar. Do I know you?"

"I'm not sure, ma'am," he said politely, waiting to see if she'd recognize him.

Francisco, who'd been standing against the wall behind them, his meaty arms folded across his broad chest, stepped forward to squint at Daniel as well. "Detectives Ibarra and Rodriguez?" he muttered, then let loose with a couple of curses. He pointed a thick finger at Daniel. "You're Rodriguez, aren't you?"

Daniel nodded calmly, his eyes hooded. Seemed like Lola would get her show after all.

Francisco slammed his hands down on the table, and it seemed like the entire house shook and rattled at the impact. He leaned forward, getting into Daniel's face. "Which one are you?"

Daniel didn't flinch, meeting Francisco's stare calmly, a small purposeful smile playing at his lips. "What do you mean?"

"Patricio or Daniel? Which one of those Rodriguez *cabrones* are you?"

Daniel waited a beat, then pushed back from the table. Coming slowly to his feet, he tugged back the hem of his suit jacket as he rested one hand on his hip, casually displaying the Glock holstered there. It was a cheesy move straight out of the movies, but it often worked. "Does it matter?"

"Paco, don't, *corazon*—" his mother began, putting one hand on her son's bare bicep. He shook her off.

"Yes," Francisco hissed, pushing his face closer to Daniel's across the table. "It matters. Because one of you killed my sister Sonia."

Daniel didn't answer. This was what they'd wanted to achieve, after all, and he'd wait for hours if it meant Francisco would dig himself a nice little hole soon.

Francisco slammed his hands against the tabletop once more, the bang reverberating through the little kitchen. "Which one are you?" he roared.

"Whoa, there, Sparky." All of Lola's peers were "Junior" and all of her potential arrestees were "Sparky" which, Daniel guessed, was actually appropriate to this case. She rose to stand beside Daniel. "We can do this the polite way, here, or you can go for a ride in our nifty squad car. What's it gonna be?"

"You're Patricio, aren't you?" Francisco lowered his voice, but his expression was one of intense fury—made more extreme

by the man's small eyes and broken nose.
"I hope he gets you," he said. "I hope you
freakin' burn."

Chapter Nine

"You hope who gets him?" Lola asked. Francisco remained perfectly still, glowering at Daniel, and he didn't say a word. Several seconds ticked by, marked by a loud clicking noise from the cat-shaped clock with the moving tail hanging near the door.

"Okay, that's it. Nifty squad car it is." Lola pulled a pair of handcuffs off her belt and clamped one end around Francisco's thick wrist. "You can tell us all about it at the station."

Francisco yanked his arm up and away. Though Lola did her best to hang on, her entire body jerked with the motion, and it was clear who was in control of the handcuff situation. "Get away from me, man!"

Francisco shouted. "I ain't going no-where!"

In a flash, Daniel was across the table. He grabbed Francisco's wrist and bent the man's hand around at an impossible angle, holding it with both of his own against his chest for leverage, until the big man was practically whimpering with pain.

"Paco, sweetie," his mother began tentatively, her forehead wrinkled with worry. She rose a few inches off her chair, then sat again, her fingers toying nervously with the ends of her scarf.

"If your brother is behind the Cobra murders, he's going away for a long time," Danny said softly, bringing his face close to Francisco's to make sure the man heard everything. "So I'd cooperate if I were you. Because Marco'll go to Pelican Bay this time, and I'll tell the D.A. to make sure you go there, too."

Francisco quieted down immediately at the mention of Pelican Bay, all the fight leaving his body. Daniel was bluffing—he had no more pull with the D.A. than the average patrol cop did, but Francisco didn't need to know that.

"It's a house of horrors up there, Paco," Daniel continued. "Makes San Quentin look like a five-star hotel. You don't want to experience it firsthand, trust me."

Francisco didn't meet Daniel's eyes, obviously well aware of Pelican Bay's gruesome reputation. "I don't know nothing," he ground out, glaring stubbornly at a spot on the floor.

"Think about it, Paco," Daniel replied, still using the same reasonable, measured tone. "We'll talk again at the station." He took the pressure off Francisco's hand, then pushed both of the man's wrists behind his back and fastened the second part of the handcuffs.

With a brief glance at Maribel Sanchez, who stood silently in a corner of her small kitchen, twisting a dish towel in her hands, Daniel left, pushing Francisco in front of him as Lola followed behind. When they reached the Crown Vic, Lola opened the back door and put her hand on top of the big man's head to get him inside. Just before Francisco was completely in, he raised his eyes and looked at Daniel.

"She was a good girl," he said.

"What?" Daniel moved closer, motioning to Lola to step aside.

"Sonia. She was a good girl. Smart." Francisco's eyes were unnaturally bright. "I still miss her sometimes." Francisco ducked his head inside and pulled his sandal-clad foot off the concrete and into the car. He straightened his body so he was staring forward out the windshield. His lips moved once more, and it took Daniel a moment to make out what he'd said.

"Why couldn't you all just leave her alone?"

Daniel pushed the door closed, smacked the roof of the car a couple of times lightly with the flat of his hand. It was a question his brother Patricio no doubt asked himself all the time, every day.

JUST AS DANIEL HAD STARTED to fold himself into the driver's seat of the Crown Vic, he noticed Maribel Sanchez wave to him from behind the screen door to her kitchen. The movement was subtle, just a flick of her hand at the level of her mid-section, and for a moment, he thought he might have imagined that she was calling him back. But then he saw her mouth the word *"ven,"* Spanish for "come," which had him veering back out of the car before he'd even had a chance to sit down.

"Lola, I'll be right back." He didn't have to tell her to keep an eye on Paco. She nodded and fastened her seat belt on the passenger side.

He took the two steps up to Maribel Sanchez's side door in one large stride, then entered her kitchen once more.

Maribel folded her arms across her chest, her hands gripping her elbows and squeezing them. Her back was bowed, and though she was tall, she looked as if she was trying to fold herself into a petite package, trying to make herself disappear. The pose was at odds with the jaunty scarf tied around her hair, the small but whimsically decorated kitchen. Daniel wondered how often she assumed that pose with her family.

"Mrs. Sanchez, is there something I can do for you?" he asked gently.

"I just—" Her face crumpled, and she ducked her head and shielded her eyes with her hand for a moment. Her shoulders shook with silent sobs.

"Uh..." Tempted to bolt for the door and let Lola handle this, Daniel stood awkwardly before Mrs. Sanchez. He reached out a hand to pat her on the shoulder and then pulled it back at the last minute, wondering how appropriate it would be to touch the woman. Damn. He'd hunted down serial killers, gone *mano a mano* with drug runners hopped up on smack, talked unstable men with guns into dropping their weapons and walking into custody. But put him face-to-face with a crying woman—or man, for that matter— and he wanted to run for the hills.

His hand jerked again toward Mrs. Sanchez, almost of its own accord, and he pulled it back, then finally reached out and patted her awkwardly on her arm. He wished he carried a handkerchief so he could give it to her. It seemed like the right thing to do in this situation, and at least it would have given him *something* to do.

"Mrs. Sanchez, if you have any idea where Marco is, it'd be better for everyone, especially Francisco," he said. "We just want to talk to him."

"I know if you are looking for Marco, it must be something bad," she said, her Spanish accent growing thicker as her stress increased. Shoulders heaving, Mrs. Sanchez took a big, gulping breath, and then she dropped her hand from her face and looked up at him with teary brown eyes. "My sons, I'm—"

Her sadness seemed to reach out and wrap itself around him, making him feel as if he were smothering. He wished he could say something, do something, to fix it, make it go away. "We just want to question Francisco. He'll probably be back home this afternoon," he said, even though he could guarantee no such thing.

"No!" She fired the word at him like a bullet. "You don't understand."

"What don't I understand?" he prompted. Maribel curved into herself even further, staring down at her hands folded across her waist.

"I am afraid of them," she whispered.

"Of your sons?"

"Sí." Hugging herself tightly, she moved to the far end of the kitchen and leaned into the corner where her cupboards formed an L. "Their father, he died in a factory accident when they were very young. I did my best, but I had to go to work, and I couldn't control them." More tears spilled down her cheeks. "They got so wild, and now that they are older, now that Marco is out of jail…" She pushed off the counter and moved to stand before him. She unbuttoned the left cuff of her light cotton shirt and pushed up the sleeve.

A series of deep, angry bruises marred the skin of her forearm just below the elbow. Daniel did touch her then, gingerly placing two fingers under her wrist and guiding her arm upward so he could see them better. Whoever did this had meant to hurt her, perhaps even break her arm. A white-hot bolt of anger shot through him, and he clenched his teeth tightly and did his best not to let it show.

"Mrs. Sanchez—"

"I will go to my sister's, in Century City. She works for a movie studio and has lots of money," she said, her voice breaking around the word *money*. "Please, just keep them away from me."

"If you come to the station, press charges against whichever one of them did this to you…" Daniel began.

"Perhaps. But first I have to give you something." She took her arm away and rolled her sleeve back down, buttoning the cuff.

Tearing a sheet off a thin notepad that hung on her refrigerator, attached by magnets on its back, Mrs. Sanchez grabbed a pen from a nearby drawer and scribbled an address on it.

"This is Marco's cousin Felix's address. I think Marco might be renting a room from him." She looked down at her hands. "He did the last time he was out of jail."

Daniel took the piece of paper from her. A quick glance at the writing on it told him that the cousin's residence was only a mile or two away from Mrs. Sanchez's home.

"Please, keep Paco for as long as you can. I will go to my sister."

"I can arrange for police protection—"

"No," she said. "My sister's house has a—how you say?—gate around it, *como un fortaleza*. Like a fortress. I will be safe."

Daniel studied Mrs. Sanchez in silence, wondering if he was being played. Mrs. Sanchez seemed eager to get rid of him, to get rid of Paco and run off to the sister in Century City. And why would one sister live in such luxury—which is what he assumed her gated community in Century City would yield—while the other lived in poverty in a not-so-nice area of East L.A.?

Then again, those bruises on Mrs. Sanchez's arm were not made by running into a door. Someone had hurt her badly.

"Will you come to the station and press charges?" he asked, afraid to hear the answer he knew was coming. A woman didn't endure abuse like that for years, only to end it without a lot of emotional back and forth, a lot of second-guessing herself.

"I will think about it," she replied.

Well, it was a start. He'd learned from too many domestic violence calls as a patrol cop that you couldn't make a woman seek help until she was ready. Reaching into his pocket, Daniel gave her his card. "This has my work number and my personal cell. Call me anytime you need anything," he said. She nodded.

It would have to do, for now. But if he had his way, in the next few hours, the Homicide Special unit would make sure neither Marco nor Francisco Sanchez would ever hurt her or anyone else, ever again.

Chapter Ten

By the time Lola had finished grilling
Francisco Sanchez, it was dark out. While
Daniel had watched through a one-way
mirror, not participating since he was officially on leave, Francisco had refused to
say another word about his brother,
Marco, and the lawyer he'd called in made
sure he didn't say much about anything
else, either. Francisco did, however, estab-
lish that he had a clear-cut alibi on the
days of both Jay and Oscar's murders.
He'd been at his gym, and though Lola
would dispatch officers to make certain,
Francisco told them he had proof in the
form of witnesses and records of his presence on security tapes. So, after what

added up to be mostly a wasted evening, Daniel called St. X to check up on Celia—who was fine—and made his way back to her Sayers Hall apartment.

When he got there, his brother Joe was standing in the hall outside Celia's door, staring down three of the West Bureau's biggest patrol cops. By his feet sat Roadkill, the ugliest mutt ever to walk the Earth, in Daniel's opinion. Roadkill was scrawny but long, with dingy white fur and liver-colored spots dotting one side of his head. The other side had one big spot covering most of it, giving him a reverse "Phantom of the Opera" look. Though the rest of his body was smooth and short-haired, his particolored head was shaggy. One side of his mouth pulled up higher than the other, giving the impression that the dog was constantly smirking at everything around him. He'd gotten his name, Joe had told Daniel, because someone had abandoned him by the side of the road as a puppy. Joe had rescued him, and he'd been Joe's faithful and butt-ugly companion for several years.

"Look, I'm a friend," Joe explained as if

talking to three small and very deficient children. Roadkill smirked up at the cops, his skinny, ropelike tail thumping lazily on the flat hallway carpeting. "Danny Rodriguez is my brother, and I know he's staying here. If you'd just let me talk to Celia—"

The cops seemed to solidify into a wall of LAPD muscle at Joe's words, making access to Celia's door all but hopeless. "I'm sorry, sir," one of them explained politely. "We have orders not to allow anyone in until Detective Rodriguez gets back. Especially not with…" The cop bent his head slightly to get a better look at Roadkill. "Is that a dog?"

"Is that a—" Joe began, a note of incredulity in his voice. One thing Daniel had learned very quickly after finding Joe several months ago was that you never, ever, ever insulted the dog. Daniel figured he'd better end this quickly.

He moved out of the stairwell and cleared his throat. "It's okay," he said. "Joe really is my brother. And the dog is my long-lost nephew, so watch the comments, Officers."

Officer Carter, a ruddy-faced man with blond hair so light, he looked as if he had no eyelashes, squinted at Joe. He'd worked with Carter several times, and the man was well-acquainted with at least part of his family history. The murders of his and Joe's birth parents, LAPD cops themselves, were still talked about by members of the LAPD—a case that had gone unsolved and had haunted the establishment until a few short months ago.

"I thought you said your twin was identical, Detective?" Carter asked.

Daniel sighed. Things always got weird when he had to start explaining his family history to people. It sounded like he was summarizing one of his mother's beloved *telenovelas*. "He's my oldest brother. We were separated by adoption." Enough said, he figured.

Carter and the other two cops made no secret of visually examining Joe, as if trying to parse out the family resemblance. It shouldn't have been that hard—all three brothers had the same pale brown eyes and sharply arched eyebrows. Joe's hair was longer and thicker, and he had their father's prominent, slightly aquiline nose, while Danny and Patricio had their mother's straight one. Joe's face was a touch wider, his eyes slightly more almond-shaped, but otherwise, the resemblance was unmistakable.

When the three cops didn't remark on it immediately, Joe took matters into his own hands. "What?" he asked. "You missed our moving reunion on the Lifetime Channel?"

Not knowing what to make of that, the cops turned to Daniel for confirmation. Carter was still squinting at Joe as if still searching for matching family traits.

"He's kidding," Daniel said. "We weren't on the Lifetime Channel."

Two of the cops just nodded, but Carter jabbed a finger at Joe as he gathered his thoughts. "You were on the news," he finally said. Ah, that's why he'd been staring. "That story about Senator Allen's wife trying to have you and your girlfriend killed."

"Fiancée," Joe clarified. He and said fiancée, Emma Jensen Reese, who also worked at St. X in the English department, had been practically incommunicado for a couple of weeks now, mired in making plans for their upcoming wedding. Even though Joe had only been in his life as an adult for a few months, Daniel had missed him.

"And Amelia Allen had your parents killed when you were kids because they were blackmailing her husband over an affair he had," Carter said, reciting the facts as they came back to him. "I saw that on Channel 7. That's really tough, man." Joe shrugged, his face carefully blank. Carter turned to Daniel. "He's related to you?"

"Older brother," Daniel repeated. Why did he have to have a past that was so *weird?*

"You were adopted?" Carter asked. He was a good guy, but damn, the man was nosy.

"Don't you have somewhere to be, Officers?" Daniel said. "I can take it from here."

The five men grunted good nights at one another, and then the officers filed through the stairwell exit, leaving him and Joe alone in the hallway.

Daniel grinned slowly at his brother. "You know, you keep rattling off about how 'moving' our story is, someone's actually going to make a TV movie out of us. You're living near Hollywood now, dude."

"Nah." Joe reached over and smacked Daniel lightly on the arm. "Too bizarre. No one would believe it."

With a laugh, Daniel turned to knock on Celia's door, then paused. "How did you find me, anyway? I didn't tell anyone where I was going."

"I'm a private investigator," Joe replied, shooting him a sideways glance. "I have my ways."

"No, really," Daniel said, his knuckles still hovering near Celia's door in mid-knock. "I haven't talked to anyone about being here."

"Called Lola," Joe said. "She adores me. She'll tell me anything."

Daniel rolled his eyes, though he knew

it must be true. Lola usually liked to sit on coveted information like a big fat dragon on a pile of jewels, just to watch people squirm. "Yeah, she's always had a soft spot for whackjobs."

"And witty, good-looking P.I.s," Joe added.

Just as Daniel was about to reply, Celia's door swung open and the lady herself popped her head outside, having finally heard the commotion outside her door. Roadkill immediately perked up, panting happily, which made him look a little less smirky.

"Good-looking P.I.s?" Celia looked directly at Joe. "You see any?"

Joe put his hand over his heart. "Aw, man, Cel, that hurts. That really hurts."

"Kidding!" Celia smiled at him, and then Darcy and Tanya, the two girls Daniel had met in the theater the other day, squeezed past her and out of the apartment. "Bye, Dr. V.," Darcy said. "Thanks for dinner. Oh, look! A dog! How cu— Uh." She bent to scratch Roadkill behind the ears. "A dog," she finished lamely, though she continued to scratch the dog's head with the same amount of enthusiasm.

"Thank you, Dr. V.," Tanya added as she came out of the apartment. "Oooh, a dog!" Tanya crouched down to join her friend and began scrubbing Roadkill's back. The dog panted harder and sat politely, in butt-ugly dog heaven. One thing he had to give Roadkill, the dog was probably the nicest one he'd ever met. Guess he had to be, with that ugly mug.

"Hey, Detective Rodriguez." Tanya looked up at him. "This your dog?" Darcy moved to scratch Roadkill's back along with Tanya.

"No, my brother's," he responded, jerking his head toward Joe.

"Can we play with him for a while?" Tanya asked Joe. "I have a dog at home— Smeagle the beagle. I. Miss. Him. So. Much." She took Roadkill's face in both her hands and rubbed behind his ears at each word, using the kind of pouty speech just shy of baby talk that some people reserved for their canine brothers and sisters.

"Sure," Joe responded, and the two girls

happily herded the dog into one of the nearby dorm rooms, their high-pitched laughter still echoing in the hallway.

Daniel raised an eyebrow at Celia, hoping that Darcy and Tanya were about to pack their things and go home to their families. "What's up with those two? I thought the students were leaving?"

Celia's mouth flattened, and she shook her head. "Darcy and Tanya are from Maine. They couldn't get a last-minute flight back home until tomorrow, and they have nowhere else to stay." She waited until the girls closed their doors. "I don't like it, either, but the only place for them to camp out was the cafeteria or the library, and they said they'd rather sleep in their own beds. It's just for one night, and Security is beefing up their patrols. With real security, not student workers."

With that, she turned to Joe, her brown eyes lighting up. "And hey, stranger, I never see you and Emma anymore. Tell me where you've been hiding her." Celia grabbed his arm and tugged him inside, with barely another glance at Daniel.

Celia was good friends with Emma, and as such, had gotten to know Joe quite well in the last few months. The first time he'd heard Joe mention Celia, Daniel had nearly jumped through the roof. Even though his brother was very, very taken, he couldn't help but feel a little jealous of Joe's easy rapport with his usually prickly ex. At least, prickly where Daniel was concerned.

After offering to fetch drinks for everyone, Celia went into the kitchen, leaving Joe and Daniel seated in her brightly colored living room.

"So, what's up?" Daniel asked without preamble. "Something made you track me down." One look at Joe's face, and Daniel knew he was right. His brother's light brown eyes were practically glittering with excitement.

"I think I might have a lead on Sabrina."

Okay, that was big. Daniel felt a bubble of emotion swell inside his chest. His baby sister. He could still remember the fat baby rolls on her chubby arms and legs, the two little teeth that had just popped through her bottom gums the last time he'd seen her. She'd been eighteen months old then, and she'd had a joyful, high-pitched laugh that made him happier than anything else in the world. He and Patricio had been five years old then, and baby Sabrina had seemed an almost magical creature.

When their parents had died, murdered over a blackmail scheme of their father's that had gone very, very wrong, the family had been torn apart. They'd had no other family, and as soon as Social Services had gotten their hands on the children, Sabrina had been adopted and taken away.

Then their big brother Joe had stopped talking, to them and to anyone, and his long silence caused him to be taken away, too. Daniel now knew that he'd been put in a foster home for wayward kids in the northern part of the state. He and Patricio had spent a long six months in foster care, until Edgardo and Felicia Rodriguez had come along. They'd adopted the twins and showered them with love, though after having everyone they ever cared about taken away from them, Daniel and Patricio had taken a long time to learn how to trust another family.

Once they were adults, they tried in vain to find Joe and Sabrina, but a fire had destroyed their adoption records, making it almost impossible to locate them. But they'd never given up, and Joe had finally found them. Sabrina was still out there, and Daniel knew he and his brothers would search for her until they were old men, if they had to.

He could still remember her laugh.

"Where?" he asked, his voice catching in his throat.

Celia silently padded across the room in her stockinged feet, setting a tray with two beers poured into frosted mugs and a glass of white wine on the coffee table. She sat down on the love seat beside Daniel, worrying her bottom lip with her teeth, her expression as anxious and hopeful as he felt.

"Since the records are gone, I decided to take a shot in the dark and hope that Sabrina's adoptive family hadn't changed her first name," Joe explained, leaning forward on the sofa to rest his elbows on his knees. "So far, I've had to limit my search to people who want their records open—who want to be found by their birth relatives, in other words. I found a Sabrina Jenkins who lives in Seattle."

Jenkins, Daniel thought. An Anglo family. Did they tell her she was Mexican and Honduran? Did they teach her anything about her culture? Did she learn Spanish, at least take it in high school? He realized how lucky he and Patricio had been to have Felicia and Edgardo, who were Mexican and had taught them much about their cultural background. They'd even taken them to Honduras on vacation when the twins were sixteen.

"So, she has the same birthday?" Daniel asked, knowing that Joe would have checked that out. Sabrina had been born on December 30, 1980.

"December 31," Joe said, and Daniel felt his hopes sink. Celia put a tentative hand on his arm.

"It's one day off from our Sabrina's," Joe

continued, "but the agency people I've talked to said that doesn't rule her out. Paperwork mistakes happen."

"Have you called her?" Celia finally broke in.

Joe shook his head. "I'm going to go to Seattle. Patricio is already there, as you know, and we thought we'd call her locally. Give her less of a chance to say no, you know?" He stared at his knuckles.

Daniel didn't say anything, but he knew that if Sabrina decided for some reason that she didn't want to meet her brothers, Joe and Patricio would probably find her, anyway, just to catch a glimpse of her. He knew that was why Joe wanted to go up to Washington before calling her. And he knew he would do the same.

"I'm going up there tomorrow," Joe said. "I know you're busy—" he shot a quick glance at Celia before continuing "—but I wanted to check with you before I left. See if…" He trailed off.

At Joe's tacit request that Danny go to Seattle with him, Celia suddenly became very absorbed in picking at her cuticles.

Her index fingernail made rapid scraping noises against the side of her thumb, wordlessly communicating her agitation. Maybe...maybe she actually didn't want him to go, despite all her efforts to convey the contrary in her every word and deed. Interesting.

Without letting Celia know he was on to her, he stood up. "Joe," he said, stretching one arm lazily over his head and holding on to its elbow with the other. "Let's go outside for a minute. I need some air."

AIR. AIR, SCHMAIR. He was going to leave her, all alone, with Marco Sanchez just waiting to fry her big Latina behind once the opportunity presented itself.

Dammit!

Celia rose and picked up Joe and Daniel's mugs off the coffee table, carrying them into the kitchen and dumping them unceremoniously into the sink. The thick glass clattered against the stainless steel as the two mugs rolled along the sink bottom. Frankly, she didn't care if they broke. They took up too much room in the dishwasher, anyway.

Heading back into the living room, she located her abandoned wineglass and downed the rest of the Australian chardonnay in two long gulps.

Better, but not much.

Alone. Alone, alone, alone.

Oh, she knew she was being ridiculous. For one, Danny wouldn't leave her by herself, at the mercy of Marco Sanchez. He'd bring back Larry, Curly and Scary to guard her door and flank her like her own Secret Service detail every time she went outside. But the thought didn't make her feel any better. Of course family came first— she knew that on an intellectual level—but in her heart, she hated the thought of his leaving her.

And two, she felt as if he was shutting her out, all over again. For one thing, she hadn't even known he *had* a baby sister until Joe and Emma had filled her in on all the details of his parents' deaths and the subsequent adoptions. That's how much he'd trusted her with the important details of his past. And now he couldn't even bring himself to finish his conversation about finding Sabrina in front of her, choosing instead to haul Joe out into the parking lot. Probably he'd just disappear now, without telling her where he was going. Probably she wouldn't see him again until the next time he wanted...

She didn't even want to think about what he wanted.

Nearly ping-ponging off the walls with pent-up, maddening energy, Celia went into her bedroom walk-in closet and started rearranging her shoes. For some reason, she sometimes found communing with her shoes soothing, and if there was ever a time where she needed Betsey Johnson and Steve Madden to calm her down, it was now.

She flipped on the closet light and walked to the back, where her shoes lined a series of shelves Oscar Valencia had kindly custom-built for her after she'd helped him get into a night-school prelaw program.

Don't think about Oscar.

She pulled down an impossibly high pair of clear plastic slides with silver marabou trim covering the uppers. Her stripper shoes, bought when she'd signed up for Strip-Tease Aerobics at an outside gym, the latest L.A. exercise craze. It had been fun, but there were never enough poles to go around because of the high demand, so she'd gone back to swimming. But the shoes…the shoes might come in handy sometime. And not with Danny Rodriguez. She placed them on the uppermost shelf, next to the wall on her left-hand side. Today, the shoes would go in rainbow order. Last time, she'd sorted them alphabetically by designer.

Or maybe the black ones should go on top. She grabbed the first pair of black shoes she saw.

They were a delicate pair of sling backs with a tiny heel, made of thick, matte nylon with satin trim that criss-crossed the upper and then twisted back around the ankle. She'd worn them to a police department benefit ball she'd gone to with Danny, just before Sonia Sanchez had died and everything had gone to hell.

She'd taken such care getting ready, buying shoes she couldn't afford on her college-student salary, finding a dress she also couldn't afford that had hugged her curves in the right places and set off her curly black hair. She'd even had one of her theater department friends do her hair and makeup, just because it was a special night, and she couldn't afford a visit to the salon because of those damn shoes. The end result had been a whole new personal best as far as her looks went—her hair blown out straight and piled on top of her head, and her makeup enhancing her huge brown eyes and playing down her wide mouth. She'd been so eager to show Danny that instead of waiting for him to pick her up, she'd taken a cab to his La Brea apartment.

When he opened the door in answer to her knock, he hadn't said a word. His face hadn't even moved.

Celia's anxious grin had faltered a little, but she knew Danny. Compliments weren't exactly his thing, but she thought he might try, given her Herculean effort.

"Well?" she prompted, doing a little

twirl in the hallway. Someone down the hall let out a faint wolf whistle.

Danny just stared at her. A slow smile spread across his face, and he bit his bottom lip, a wicked gleam in his golden eyes. She knew that look. It was a good look, a look that usually got her right in the knees. But tonight, she wanted—no, she deserved more.

"How do I look?" she asked impatiently.

Daniel reached for her, pulling her to his chest. His hands made slow, lazy circles on the small of her back as he made it clear he intended to kiss her.

Tonight, that wasn't enough. "No, Danny." She pressed her palms flat against his chest. "How do I *look?*"

He lowered his eyelids and brought his mouth down to hers.

"Mmrph." She pushed him away again, arching her back to keep her face away from his. "Daniel Ramon Rodriguez, answer the question."

"Uh…"

This was not going well.

"Good," he said finally. "You look good."

She glared at him.

"Nice?" He hooked a finger under his collar and tugged. "Really nice?"

"You're pathetic, Rodriguez." With that, she pushed past him and moved to sit on his ratty couch, the only furniture in his entire living room besides the cheap, particle-board television stand and state-of-the-art TV.

She'd let it drop then, hadn't let it ruin her evening. But on a microcosmic scale, that moment had taught her an important lesson that had been driven home over the years. Danny was always ready with a compliment or an emotional detail when he wanted something—namely, her. Like that time a year and a half ago when she'd had a terrific lapse in judgment after her Latin ballroom class. He doled it out in little bits and pieces, but he never opened up when it really mattered. He'd shut her out completely when Patricio was dealing with the Sanchez murder, and he'd shut her out again when Joe had come over with the news about Sabrina.

Celia would always be second to his

family, when all she'd wanted was to be part of his family, and to welcome him into hers. But, maybe some things weren't meant to be.

"Stupid shoes," she said, flinging the sling backs into the nether reaches of her closet, hoping to fling the memory with it. "Stupid, emotionally unavailable jerk." She reached for the next pair.

"Now, I know you can't be talking about me," someone drawled behind her. She whirled around to see Danny standing in the doorway of her closet. And he had that look in his eye again.

"YOU'RE BACK," SHE SAID, before she could stop herself.

He blinked. "What did you think, I was going to leave you?"

Ignoring the fact that they were in her closet—a smaller, much more intimate space than she would have cared to share with him at that moment—Celia folded her arms and looked him square in the eye. "Well, yeah, I did, Holmes."

"Why?"

Such a simple question, but it would take forever to answer. Then again, "forever" had never stopped Celia before. "Because you finally have a lead on your sister after years of searching. Because family comes first. Because the three amigos you left here while you ran off with Detective Ibarra are not only perfectly acceptable when it comes to protection, but they're probably better than the president's security detail. Because things would probably be better if you left."

Daniel didn't say anything, just stared at her with those unreadable, otherworldly eyes.

Celia picked up a shoe—a siren-red pump—and cradled it for comfort, pretending to examine it for scuffs. "Because you always leave."

In less than a second, he was standing before her, taking the shoe out of her grasp. "I've never wanted to leave," he said. "You always ask me to leave."

He was standing so close, too close, and she didn't think she could take being in such a small space with him anymore. She tried to move around him, but he blocked her way. "Talk to me, Cel."

"No." Her head jerked up. "You talk to me. You close yourself off all the time. Did you know that until Joe told me, I didn't even know you'd had a sister? And we've known each other since we were kids." Then she did push past him, her body brushing against his in a way that felt so good, and so painful. She stalked into her bedroom, and Danny followed.

"We've been down this road before, Danny," she continued. "We always seem to come back to each other, hurt each other, and I don't know why we can't just have a clean break after all these years."

"Maybe we're not meant to have a break at all," he said calmly. "Maybe that's why we keep coming back to each other."

Celia shook her head, feeling the sharp pang of tears behind her eyes. Good, maybe she should cry. That was a surefire way to make Danny run in the opposite direction.

"I've had a full and wonderful life since we broke up," she said, and God help her,

her hands were shaking. "I barely think of you. And yet, when I see you, it's—" She stopped, swallowed sharply. "I feel like something's been missing, and then it just hurts to look at you."

Danny stepped forward and took her in his arms, and heaven help her, it felt like coming home.

"Then close your eyes," he said softly, and his mouth came down on hers.

Their kiss stayed gentle for only a fraction of a second, and then the familiar rush that was Daniel Rodriguez took over her senses. She buried her hands in his short, dark hair, and she was practically gasping as their kisses turned rough, desperate. Oh, it had been so long....

"Celia," he murmured against her lips. Tossing the shoe he held onto the ground, he ran his hand down her spine, cupping her behind with one hand.

She wasn't sure how it happened, but her legs ended up wrapped around his waist in one effortless movement, and she felt as if she couldn't get close enough to him. "Danny," she whispered, cupping his beautiful face in her hands, her hair falling around them. "I want you. I always want you. So much." He was like a drug. Every intelligent fiber in her body knew this wouldn't end well, but that intelligence was swiftly being replaced. And she didn't care, as long as he never stopped touching her.

He pressed her against the wall next to the closet door, and she barely registered the doorjamb bisecting her back. He lowered his head and devoured her neck, and she couldn't think or feel anything anymore except Danny's mouth, Danny's hands....

Unhooking her legs, she slid down his body in one exquisite, burning movement, and then they were on the floor. They ended up on a pile of scarves and shawls Celia had been sorting just inside her closet, and Danny was on top of her, his body firm, hard, graceful in its every movement. If it hadn't been for the fact that they were still clothed, he would have been inside her.

The thought made her burn.

Gripping the hem of his T-shirt, Celia

tugged the fabric upward, until Danny rose up above her and shucked it in one smooth movement that took her breath away. She ran her hands across the skin of his well-muscled chest, and she just didn't feel like she'd ever get close enough to him.

"*Me has hecho falta*, Celia," he whispered, taking her earlobe in between his teeth, making her gasp and arch into him. "*Yo siempre te hecho de menos.*"

I've missed you, Celia. I always miss you.

Nothing, no one, ever made her feel like this, and in the foggy haze that was her mind, she wondered why she'd ever thought letting Danny go was a good idea.

He made short work of the button fly of her jeans, and then he was yanking them off her body, his mouth on hers once more. When they reached her ankles, she kicked them off in one smooth movement and then peeled off her pink T-shirt, exposing the peach-and-ivory lace La Perla bra she'd splurged on recently.

He froze, inhaling sharply.

She tried to pull his head back down to

hers. "Danny," she sighed. She probably should have felt self-conscious, since she was mostly naked and he still wore his jeans, but she didn't. She never did around him. "Danny," she whispered again.

Slowly, almost reverently, he dropped his head to place a light kiss on her collarbone, then another just below. "We always do this, Cel," he said. "We always tear at each other as if we're starving."

Celia took a deep, shuddering breath, not quite knowing where he was going.

"Not here." His golden eyes practically smoldered, but he was a study in self-control. "Not in your closet, not on your floor." He tipped her chin up with his fingers and brushed her mouth lightly with his. "I want you on your bed, and this time, I'm going to take my time." He brushed his cheek against hers, nuzzled her neck, bit her earlobe softly. Then he kissed her, sucking lightly at *the* spot on her neck near her hairline, and she gasped, clinging to him. An exquisite chill rippled across her skin.

He laughed softly. "I know you," he

whispered as she clung to him. "I know what makes you crazy. I know what makes you sigh, and I know exactly how to make you scream for me. And I'm going to do it all, tonight in your bed." He plunged his hand into her hair, bending her head back to expose the other side of her neck. "Again." He kissed the hollow at her throat. "And again." His hand skimmed up the inside of her bare leg as he kissed the swell of her breast, leaving goose bumps in its wake. "And again." Just as his fingers reached her bikini line and his mouth went to the edge of her bra, he pulled away. She couldn't have moved or even spoken if she'd tried. She could barely breathe.

He moved out of her arms and stood then, magnificent in the early evening light. He held his hand out to her. "Come here, Celia, *mi amor,*" he said.

Silently, she reached for him, and he pulled her up to stand before him. He kissed her one more time, then reached down to scoop her up in his arms. He carried her to her bed, deposited her gently on the sheets, and then he fulfilled every one of the promises he'd just made to her. Again, and again, and again.

SOMETIME IN THE MIDDLE of the night, Celia slipped out of her bed, unable to sleep. Her body felt amazing, but her mind was going around in circles.

She'd just slept with Danny. Again.

And as wonderful as that experience was, she knew it didn't get them any closer to closure, one way or the other.

Then again, maybe she should just enjoy the feeling, the moment, and let later take care of later.

Lifting her silk robe off the small chintz chair by the window, she wrapped it around her body. Light from the moon and the street lamps outside cast the room in multiple shades of blue, and since she was able to see so well, she looked at Danny. She'd thought he was still asleep, but then she realized his eyes were wide open, and he was watching her. In one fluid movement, he sat up, the sheet pooling around his flat stomach, leaving his sculpted chest bare. If she could have froze that moment, she would have. She could have looked at Danny like that forever.

Celia's hand wandered up to tamp down her messy curls, and she smiled at him, feeling better than she had in days. Months, even. She started toward him.

"You're beautiful," he said.

His words stopped her cold. All of the old feelings, old questions, old doubts came shooting to the surface.

"You only tell me that when you want me," she said, and the words were a revelation when said out loud. "You only let me glimpse a little bit of what's going on inside of you when we're crazy with wanting each other. Why is that, Danny?"

"You left me, Cel," he said. "I tried a thousand times to get you back, to just get you to talk to me." He raked his hand through his close-cropped hair, blew out a hard breath. "You think all those times we got together after we broke up were just hookups? I wanted you in my life again. Every time."

How was she supposed to take that? It went against everything she'd believed about him, about them, for the past eleven years. Damn the man, if he could have just said those words earlier.... "That's the first time you've ever admitted that to me," she countered.

"Once again, can we remember that you left me?" His voice actually rose from its usual soft, intense modulation. Now he was sort of loud and intense, which seemed strange coming from him.

"I know. But Danny, I tried so many times to tell you, to show you that I was there to help you with your brother—whom I adored, by the way—but no-o-o-o. Not only did you brush me off every time, you disappeared. For over a year. Forgive me if I wasn't sitting around, waiting for you to walk back into my life when you finally came back. Forgive me if that hurt so much, I couldn't trust you."

Daniel's jaw worked, a sure sign that he was angry. "He was my brother, and he was dying. I'd do it again."

"I know," she said. *That's the problem.*

"I can't do this." Tossing the sheet angrily aside, he rose from the bed, giving her one last glimpse of his amazing body before pulling his jeans on. He kept his back to her. "You're making a fool out of me, Cel."

She couldn't believe they were having this argument again. Every time they saw each other, they played this same scene out, as if they were ghosts drawn to one place and one series of actions that they couldn't let go of.

She opened her mouth to say something, anything that would end this painful conversation, and then she stopped. The smell of burning wood had permeated the room, so subtly, she hadn't even noticed until her stomach had started to recoil in protest. "Danny—" she began, but he was already striding toward her closed bedroom door.

Then the fire alarm went off.

Chapter Eleven

Sanchez.

Positive that this was no false alarm, Daniel touched his hands to Celia's wooden bedroom door to see if it was hot.

Not yet. He opened the door, thankful that the rest of Celia's apartment appeared clear as well, though he could catch the faintest scent of smoke coming from somewhere else in the building. He turned and reached a hand toward her, their aborted conversation all but forgotten as he concentrated on getting them out of the building alive. "Come on, Celia." He hoped, God he hoped that Sanchez wouldn't be waiting for them when they opened the apartment door, hell-bent on keeping them inside, watching them burn.

Before he could stop her, Celia slipped past him and ran barefoot toward the apartment exit. "Darcy and Tanya," he heard her murmur as she pushed past him.

He lunged for her, but the smooth satin of her robe slid through his fingers like liquid. *Oh, God, Celia.*

"No!" he shouted as she pulled open the door. He half expected to see Sanchez, towering over her, pushing her back inside, dropping one of his lethal homemade bombs at her feet. But there was nothing except a river of black, churning smoke that tumbled along the ceiling. Daniel raced to the doorway.

Ahead of him, Celia stumbled, coughing, down the dark hallway. The main hallway lights weren't on, though the red exit signs at the ends provided a degree of illumination. The combination of hazy smoke and red, flickering light made Sayers Hall look like some collegiate dimension of hell.

Daniel caught up to Celia in two strides, pulling her around to face him. The building fire alarm clanged loudly, making it hard to hear anything else, so Daniel just said "Sanchez!" as loud as he could, hoping the simplicity of his statement would make her understand just how foolhardy rushing ahead was.

Apparently, his message took. Celia's eyes widened, but then she jerked her body out of his grasp, seemingly bent on heading toward the end of the hall where the smoke was at its thickest. They couldn't see the fire yet, but Daniel had no doubt that if she tried to go out that exit, she'd meet it head-on.

Then again, if she tried the south exit, behind them, Sanchez might just be there waiting for them.

"Darcy and Tanya!" she yelled.

"Where?" he replied.

As she pointed toward one of the many oak doors that lined the hallway, it opened, and Darcy stumbled out, wearing only a gray cotton camisole and a pair of boxers.

Darcy covered her ears to block out the jarring noise from the alarm, and then she noticed Celia and Daniel. Darcy tried to speak, but the loud clanging drowned out her words, though Daniel could clearly see that she was saying something about Tanya. Finally, Darcy just turned and ran down the hall to another door and started banging on it violently.

The air grew thicker as the smoke that had been mostly near the ceiling began to drift down toward the floor, filling the long hall. Daniel covered his nose and mouth with his hand, smoke searing his lungs. Celia pressed a palm to her chest, taking deep, gulping breaths that left her coughing in their aftermath. As she pounded on what had to be Tanya's door, intermittently trying the knob in a futile attempt to open the locks, Darcy coughed violently.

Moving to stand beside Darcy, Daniel cast a glance at the north exit, the one behind which the fire was most likely doing its damage. Smoke was pouring from every available crevice around, under and above the door, and he knew it was only a matter of minutes before the fire broke through to where they were standing.

Turning back to Tanya's door, he pounded on it with all his strength.

"She's impossible to wake up," Darcy shouted tearfully as she banged on the wood with her small fists. "Tanya!"

Sweeping his arm out to gently push Darcy out of the way, Daniel backed up a couple of steps, eyeing the door carefully. Then, with a deep breath, he kicked it just above the handle. Once, twice...

The door swung open, and Tanya still lay on her bed, sleeping peacefully, despite the fact that the alarm had to be twice as loud now that her door wasn't muffling it. In two steps, Daniel moved across the small, single-person dorm room, and he quickly scooped the sleeping girl up in his arms.

Celia was beside him in a flash. She patted Tanya's cheeks. "Tanya, *levántese!* Wake up!" she shouted.

Sleepily, Tanya raised her head slightly and opened one eye. "Wha...?"

Celia helped him set the girl down, her blond curls tumbling riotously all over her head and into her eyes. Her rumpled cotton pajamas had cows dancing all over them—a stupid thing for him to notice given their situation. Darcy squeezed in between them and grabbed her friend by the shoulders, shaking her. "There's a fire, you dork!" she shouted, so loudly that her every word rang out over the alarm.

Now both of Tanya's eyes were open. She still looked a little glassy and moved as if her body was stiff with years of unuse, but at least she was able to shuffle forward on her own steam. With Darcy on one side and Celia on the other, they dragged her down the hall, away from the worst of the smoke toward the south exit, Daniel leading the way. They crouched as low as possible, coughing and gasping all the way.

Through irritated, watery eyes, Daniel watched each of the doors that lined the hallway carefully as their group approached and passed them. Sanchez had to be here, somewhere, Daniel knew. The man had single-handedly killed three very strong ex-Cobras, immobilizing them and then making sure they burned alive. Daniel had no doubt he hadn't just cut and run after setting Sayers Hall ablaze.

Daniel and the women crouched as low as possible, coughing and gasping all the way, in an attempt to keep away from the worst of the smoke. He passed a set of doors, one on each side. The women came behind them.

Nothing.

They made it past another set. Daniel glanced behind them, but all of the doors they'd passed remained closed.

Sanchez, where are you?

Finally, they passed Celia's door, reaching the end of the hallway. The exit door was cool to the touch, so Daniel opened it, and the group moved inside. Thankfully, the smoke wasn't as thick here as it had been in the hall.

The dorm rooms were on the fourth floor, with the other three floors being used as classrooms. Daniel grabbed the metal rail and looked down the stairwell.

Nothing.

Where are you?

They started down. Though the alarm

was still audible in the stairwell, it was slightly less piercing, and Daniel had no problem hearing Tanya's gasping "Oh, my God!" when they reached the first landing. He spun around, his hand going for his gun, sure that Marco Sanchez had finally materialized behind them.

"Mia Finley!" Overcome by a fit of coughing that stopped whatever she was going to say next, Tanya bent double, her hands over her mouth. Daniel willed her with all his might to stop coughing and finish her sentence, because he had a bad feeling that someone was still inside the burning dorm.

Darcy thumped Tanya on the back. "Mia went home to Honolulu on a red-eye last night," she shouted at Celia.

Still bent over, Tanya started shaking her head violently, her curls tumbling from side to side.

"What?" Celia crouched low so she was eye level with Tanya, her voice a lower, huskier version of its usual sound. "Mia didn't leave?"

Swiping at her watering eyes, Tanya

straightened, still gasping for air. She bobbed her head up and down. "Flight..." She coughed, swallowed. "...cancelled. She came back." Clearing her throat roughly, she glanced at Darcy. "After you went to sleep."

"Which room?" Daniel demanded. Celia gave him a number that told him Mia's door was uncomfortably close to the side of the building where the fire had started. He had to go back.

But he couldn't leave Celia. Not when Marco Sanchez might be waiting for her.

Accurately reading his indecision, Celia put her hand on his bare arm. "We have to find Mia," she said. "She's in a wheelchair. She can't manage the stairs. I'll send Darcy and Tanya down."

Shaking his head, Daniel crossed his arm over his bare chest and covered Celia's hand with his own. "Get them out. Get them safe," he said, sparing only a glance for Darcy and Tanya, who stood waiting for them to make a decision about their friend. "I'll go."

"No—" Celia blurted, but Daniel stopped her with his words.

"They're counting on you to keep them

safe," he said. "I'll find Mia, and I'll bring her to you. I promise."

Celia looked down the spiraling stair-well, with so many corners and curves where someone could hide, and then she turned back to Daniel. "I—" He could see she was wavering.

"Keep them safe," he said. He bent forward and pressed a hard, quick kiss on her lips. God, protect this woman. He couldn't even think about what it would be like to lose her. "Be careful." He didn't have to tell Celia of whom.

With one last look at him, she put her arms around Darcy and Tanya and started down the stairs. And he started climbing. CLINGING TO DARCY AND Tanya so she wouldn't lose them in the dim light filter-ing through the rippled-glass windows above each landing, Celia crept slowly down the stairs. Her heartbeat thrumming in her ears, she couldn't make herself go any faster, despite the fact that the two young women were pulling against her grip, raring to scurry down the remaining flights and exit the building.

But Celia wouldn't let them. She reined them back in every time they started moving too fast, and now, now that they were about to reach their first blind corner, she slowed down even more.

Oh, God.

Holding her breath, Celia stepped forward, turned with the banister, looked down.

Empty.

"Dr. V.?" one of the young women prodded. She didn't know which one had spoken—all she cared about was making it down one more step alive.

How did he do it? How did he kill Oscar, Jay—both strong men who knew how to protect themselves? Oscar had been muscular from lifting weights and boxing at a local gym on the weekends. Jay had been wiry and fast. Who could have overpowered them so totally?

And did three women with ballet and gymnastics training and a smattering of campus self-defense classes stand a chance against someone like that?

Celia stumbled as she hit the next landing unaware, still expecting to find another stair beneath her. Darcy and Tanya caught her as she realized where they were.

Another blind corner.

Still clinging to the two women, she took a shuddering breath. Seeming to sense her fear, they didn't question her slow pace but remained silent. The bell of the alarm clanged loudly around them, ringing in their ears, making it hard for Celia to think.

Step forward. Turn.

The merest hint of a shadow flitted along the stairwell below. Celia motioned with her hands for Darcy and Tanya to stay put, and then she moved to the banister to look down.

There. An unmistakable movement.

She could hear him breathing.

How did you do it? she wondered. Subdue them with your body, honed into fighting condition from years of workouts in San Quentin? Attack them from behind? Take them down with a weapon, a gun?

A million ways to die, and one of them was waiting for her on the stairs below— she knew it, she felt it.

Trust your intuition, Celia Inez.

She turned to look at Darcy and Tanya. Two young women, someone's daughters, entrusted to her care by their parents and the university. She had to get them down those stairs. It was the only way out.

But she had no doubt that Marco Sanchez wouldn't just let them go. Not after they'd seen his face, watched him kill Celia.

The heat inside the stairwell had been barely noticeable when they'd first stepped inside, but now it was starting to border on unbearable. Sweat rolled down her temples and made her robe stick uncomfortably to her skin. She had to get them out of there, away from the fire above them. She had to choose.

The shadow shifted, breathed. In and out. Waiting.

Celia turned and ran back up the stairs, pulling the girls behind her.

AS SOON AS HE REENTERED the hallway, Daniel knew the fire had broken through the door on the far end. The smoke was thicker than any he'd ever seen, and he had to drop to the floor and crawl to avoid passing out from the lack of oxygen. He wondered whether Celia and her students would get out, whether Marco Sanchez was indeed waiting for them at the bottom of the stairwell. He wondered how close the fire department was to the campus— the more time Marco took to get to Celia, the more likely he'd be interrupted before he could harm her, when firefighters would swarm the building. He wondered whether Mia really was still in her room, or whether he'd die looking for her. He wondered if Celia would miss him.

But mostly, he just crawled, as fast as he could.

As he got to the halfway point of the hall, he could see an orange light flickering through the smoke. The north door was burning, and soon the entire hall would be engulfed in flames.

He kept going, counting doors. The heat grew more and more intense the closer he got to the burning end of the hallway, and when he finally reached

Mia's room, he could feel the hairs on his arms smoldering.

He pounded on the door, calling Mia's name as he crouched against the warm wood. But, as had been the case with Tanya earlier, there was no answer. Taking as deep a breath as he could without searing his lungs, Daniel stood and tried to kick the door in, just as he'd done with Tanya's. It didn't budge. He kicked it again, but it wouldn't give, maybe because the heat was making the wood swell. He tried once more, slamming the door with his shoulder and side rather than kicking it, but even that didn't get any results.

Swearing to himself in Spanish, Daniel pulled his gun out of the back of his jeans, where he'd tucked it while he'd been crawling on the floor. He always hated shooting in locks—one false move, and you could hurt someone inside. But Mia's door wasn't giving him much of a choice. Clicking off the safety, he aimed carefully and pulled the trigger. Thank God, his aim was true and the door swung open.

Inside, a young woman sat in a wheelchair near her window, her short hair tousled wildly about her head. She turned as Danny approached her, her eyes wide with fear. One hand clenched the armrest of her chair, the other still holding on to the wheel.

"I can't open the window. It's stuck!" she cried, hysteria in her voice. "The elevators aren't working. I can't get down."

Daniel ran to her side, bending low to put one arm around her shoulders, the other under her knees. "I'm going to get you out of here," he said, and she raised her arms, completely trusting him to carry her to safety.

He paused, wondering whether he'd hurt her if he lifted her the wrong way.

"I'm okay," she said, and he bent low, allowing her to wrap her arms around his neck and lifting her out of her chair.

"The window—" Mia began as he straightened, but she wasn't able to finish.

The glass of Mia's window shattered as a huge, hulking shadow punched his arm through it from the outside. Daniel didn't need to move any closer to recognize the person to whom that arm belonged.

Sanchez.

Chapter Twelve

"Dr. V.!" Obviously bewildered by her sudden movement back in the direction of the fire, Darcy and Tanya grabbed at Celia, trying desperately to get her to go back down. "What are you doing?" Darcy cried.

Spinning around, Celia put all the authority she could manage into her face and voice. "Someone started this fire on purpose," she said, "and he's down there waiting for us. I don't care if you never listen to a thing I say again, but listen to me now. We have to find another way out."

The two girls looked at each other.

"Move!" Celia yelled, pointing with an outstretched arm to the top of the stairs. It wasn't her style to yell at students like

that, but thank God, it worked this time, and they moved. She could apologize for shrieking at them later, when they were outside and still alive.

They took the stairs two at a time, scurrying back up toward the top of the building and the fire. If the history department lounge on the second floor was still open, Celia figured she could possibly get them out of this.

They burst through the second-floor hallway door, and this floor, like the one they had just come from, was filled with smoke. Celia's lungs ached, the insides of her nostrils felt scorched, and she was forced to feel her way down the hall, since she couldn't see anything. She felt Darcy and Tanya's hands, one on each of her shoulders, and she felt comforted by the touch. It told her that they were still with her, still alive.

With the girls holding on to her, Celia lurched down the dark, smoke-filled hall, stumbling and flailing for something, anything, that would give them a clue as to where they were in the building. She couldn't see, had no idea where they were, and she wondered whether she was leading them down to their deaths. *Oh, God, not here. Not like this.*

The hall seemed endless, and every doorknob her hands found wouldn't turn, locked against her frantic fingers. One of the young women was starting to wheeze, and the smoke was making her feel light-headed as well.

Celia shut her eyes tightly and opened them again, willing herself to stay focused, stay awake. Keep them alive, just a little longer. *The lounge will be open, you just have to find it.* She didn't want to think about what could be behind them, focusing instead on finding the lounge somewhere before them. So many doors. God, she hoped they hadn't passed it, because they couldn't go back. Not toward him.

Finally, Celia's flailing left hand smacked into something standing near the wall. She ran her palm across the object, feeling its smooth, rounded exterior, cool to the touch, even in this heat.

The water cooler that marked the entrance to the history department head's office and department lounge. Thank God.

It took only a moment for her fingers to find the door. She reached for the brass knob and turned it, and to her relief, the door opened. Celia pushed into the room, taking Darcy and Tanya with her.

At the far end of the room was a large window, outside of which was a small, ornately carved stone balcony. The old brownstone building boasted a handful of those balconies, which were randomly placed on its outer walls. Rumor had it there used to be more, but the university had taken the ones off the dorm rooms because the balconies were notoriously unstable, liable to crumble off the side of the building and send any adventurous students on them careening toward the ground.

But the gamble beat staying inside, with a fire and a vengeful killer on the loose.

Unhooking the latch, Celia shoved the window upward with a grunt. At first it wouldn't budge, but after several tries, it finally opened in a cascade of dust and flaking paint. The three of them stuck their heads through the opening and gulped cool, clean, smoke-free air. Rejuvenated somewhat, Celia guided the rest of her body outside and then pulled her legs through, until she was standing on the balcony.

So far, so good. It hadn't fallen yet. She held out her hands toward the two young women.

"Uh…" Darcy stuck her head through the window and looked around. There wasn't much to look at, since the balconies were stone structures with solid, waist-high walls with no openings. You had to stand up on one to see the campus below.

Celia looked over the side. Way below. She swallowed and looked back at Darcy.

"Are you sure this is such a good idea, Dr. V.?" Darcy asked.

Well, no, but it was the best she could do. It was either that or burn to death. Or they could roam the halls and be chased by a murdering psychopath. At least this way, they were well hidden and stood a chance of being spotted and rescued by the fire department, whose sirens Celia could finally hear approaching in the distance. She wondered how long it had taken someone to notice Sayers Hall was ablaze and call the fire department. With most of the students and faculty gone, she supposed it was a miracle they'd been noticed this early at all.

"Darcy!" She motioned impatiently for the young woman to stop hesitating and join her on the balcony. Taking a deep breath, Darcy closed her eyes and folded her thin, tall frame through the window, emerging next to Celia on the other side. Tanya followed suit.

And they were still standing. Not a creak or a crumble in sight. The balcony was holding. Celia closed the window behind them, hoping that if the shadowy figure on the stairs was looking for them, he wouldn't even notice there was a balcony out there at all.

The window shut, Celia looked around for a tree, a ledge they could use to make getting down easier. There was nothing, so she resigned herself to simply waiting. Fortunately, from their vantage point, Celia could see a fire truck pulling into the main gate and making its way to the parking lot below.

Waving frantically, Darcy and Tanya started to shout. Celia decided not to mention that she'd felt the balcony tremble with the movement.

MARCO SANCHEZ UNWRAPPED the thick towel from around the arm he'd used to break the window. Tossing it to the ground, he stood to reveal a muscular, stocky frame well over six feet tall. Marco had always been a big guy, Daniel remembered, but prison had built him into a zero-body-fat fighting machine.

Jeez, the man just couldn't be short and stumpy like his brother, could he?

He lowered Mia back in her chair. Do-or-die time.

Sanchez laughed. "You gonna take me, Rodriguez?" he asked, his voice low and gravelly and not at all what Daniel remembered. Firelight from the hallway flickered on Marco's face, briefly illuminating a shiny scar that slashed across his throat. Ah.

"Nine years in prison," Sanchez continued, "and you think a scrawny cop like you has the *cojones* to fight me and win?"

Daniel gently pushed Mia out of the way. God, let him win, let him get her out of here.

"I don't think," he said to Sanchez. "I know."

Sanchez laughed again, then spit on the floor. "Here's what I think of you and your threats, Patricio."

Sanchez thought Daniel was his twin, the brother Marco had threatened to kill.

Nice.

Daniel chose not to correct him, figuring the mistaken identity would buy Celia some time. He clicked his tongue, loosening his stance so he'd be ready when Marco made his move. "Didn't your mother teach you not to spit in the house?"

"Didn't your mother teach you not to kill teenage girls?" Marco asked. He sidled slowly to the left.

Daniel shifted to the right, and the two

men circled each other. "I didn't kill her, Marco," he said.

"Yeah, that's what your fancy lawyer said," Marco responded. "Seven of you stood by while my sister died, powerless to stop the other two." He scowled then, his expression a mixture of fury and a still-potent grief. "*Seven* of you! And they put me in jail."

The man was right—his sister had died while most of the ex-Cobras stood by. But Patricio, the real Patricio, had come home that day with a black eye and a cracked rib after trying to save Sonia. Unfortunately, Marco would never recognize that. Just as he would never recognize that he had no right to be a one-man judge, jury and executioner.

"You tried to kill a man, Marco," Daniel said softly. "The penalty for that is prison."

Marco lunged, a lightning-fast movement that happened in a blur and ended with Daniel feeling a sharp, piercing pain in his back as Marco slammed his body against the wall. Marco shoved his forearm against Daniel's throat, pushing Daniel's head back at an awkward angle as he cut off his air. Daniel coughed and gagged. Marco loosened his hold just a little, just enough for Daniel to breathe again.

Mia screamed from her chair. Flames from the hall licked the edges of the doorway, and Daniel felt sweat trickle down the back of his neck from the intense heat in the room.

"I can't—" Marco broke off and blew out a breath, obviously frustrated. He turned his head to glance at Mia. "Get her out of here," he ground out.

Taking advantage of Sanchez's distraction, Daniel slipped his fist behind the arm Marco held against his throat, connecting with the man's chin in a sharp uppercut. Marco's head snapped back and he let go of Daniel, and Daniel followed up with a left hook. Marco stumbled across the room toward the burning hallway, knocking a couple of porcelain figurines that had sat on a low-lying table to the ground.

Just as he reached the door, Marco turned back. Swiping his bleeding mouth with the back of one hand, the man glared at Danny. "You're looking in the wrong place," he said, his gravelly voice even more hoarse from the smoke that was now pouring into the room. And then he turned away and disappeared down the hallway.

Though Daniel was tempted to follow, to stop Sanchez once and for all, he knew he couldn't leave Mia alone in her room. Not with the fire just this side of a raging inferno. Once again, he scooped her up in his arms, and he headed for the south stairwell, the one exit to the building that gave them a chance to escape. He could only hope that Sanchez wouldn't change his mind and come back.

THE LOS ANGELES FIRE Department managed to bring Celia, Darcy and Tanya off of their two-story-high perch using one of the ladders connected to their big trucks. Celia insisted that the girls go first, and as soon as she herself hit the ground, she clutched at the sleeve of the nearest firefighter and told him about Mia and how Danny had gone back upstairs to save her.

As she watched the hoses spray water on the north side of Sayers Hall, flames flickering through the windows of much of the top floor where her students' rooms were, Celia worried. And prayed.

She hadn't seen him or Mia when they'd come charging back up the stairs. She couldn't see him now that she was on the ground, despite the fact that she'd been pacing around the building—or as much of it as the firefighters would let her near—for the past several minutes after successfully fending off the paramedics who were tending to Darcy and Tanya. She'd told the firefighters about the person lingering in the south stairwell, but so far, they'd been going up and down that staircase without a hitch.

And without running into Daniel.

She steepled her hands in front of her mouth. "Please let him be okay," she breathed into her fingers. The crowd around her was growing larger—police, paramedics, firefighters moving everywhere, interviewing witnesses who'd come out of nearby buildings to see what all the fuss was about. She turned, hoping to catch a glimpse of something that would tell her how to find him.

And then the crowd parted briefly and Daniel was standing just a few feet away. His face and chest were coated with ash and sweat, and he looked as exhausted as she felt. But he was here, he was whole.

Nearly sobbing, Celia wove through the people between them, Danny doing the same, and when they were finally next to each other, she reached up and wrapped her arms tightly around him, not ever wanting to let go.

"Oh, God, Danny, I thought you were still in there." She buried her face in the hollow just beneath his shoulder, and the rush of emotion she felt astonished her.

He clung to her, his hands on her back, on her shoulders, in her hair. "Celia," he murmured. "Celia."

They remained like that for several minutes, and she just let herself enjoy the feel of him, appreciate the fact that he was all right as chaos erupted around them. And then, Celia heard someone clear his or her throat behind them.

Pulling herself out of Danny's arms, Celia found herself face to giant glasses with Detective Ibarra.

"Okay, Junior," she said without missing a beat, pretending that she hadn't seen their display of big emotion. "Someone told me Marco Sanchez was in that building when it started to burn."

Danny nodded. "He was."

"Tell me everything that happened, and make it quick," she said. "Antonio Rincon is missing. A couple of students left in Aquinas Hall where he lives reported hearing arguing coming from his room half an hour ago." She glanced up at Sayers Hall, then back at Danny and Celia. "If what happened to Oscar Valencia and Jay Alvarez is any indication, we only have about an hour left to find him alive."

Chapter Thirteen

Antonio Rincon was missing.

"You're looking in the wrong place," Marco Sanchez had said.

Of course they had been. They'd been so distracted by the fire, they hadn't even noticed how he'd let them go, how he'd moved on to Aquinas Hall and had subdued the third ex-Cobra who'd worked on the St. X campus. Apparently, after a few days of nothing happening, Rincon had demanded that his police protection leave him alone, and alone was exactly what he had been when Sanchez had come for him.

Daniel told Lola exactly what had happened, from the moment when he and Celia had first smelled smoke to a slightly abridged version of how he'd carried Mia on his back down the stairs, after Marco had vanished down the hall without a trace.

"So, Sanchez was in the student's room with you, which he entered from the window, having accessed that from the outside ledge," Lola droned. Daniel nodded. "Why come in the window at all? Why not come through the door?"

"Surprise?" Daniel said. "He probably saw me go in or heard me shoot the locks."

"Hmm." Lola turned to Celia. "And while this was happening, you said you saw someone you assumed was Sanchez waiting at the bottom of the stairwell?"

Celia shrugged. "You know, I thought I did, but I was also scared out of my head and might have been seeing things." Even as she said it, she knew, she *knew* that that wasn't the case. There had been someone waiting for them at the bottom of the stairs, and every fiber of her being told her that person had meant to do her harm. Nothing could have made her take Darcy and Tanya back up toward the fire otherwise. Nothing.

"Or he could have brought a friend to help him out." Scribbling notes in her handheld notebook, Lola twisted her mouth into a frown. "Wasn't Francisco," she told Danny. "We've still got him under surveillance."

"That," Celia agreed, not having considered the possibility of a second person before, "or he just went back to the fourth floor after Darcy, Tanya and I slipped away from him."

She answered a few more of Lola's questions, and then, when the woman turned to go, Celia stopped her with a question of her own.

"Do you think Antonio is still alive?"

"I hope so." Lola slid her pen into the wire spiral holding her notebook together. "Here's what doesn't fit, Junior. According to the guards at San Quentin, Marco Sanchez morphed into a model prisoner sometime during his last two years there. Got his GED, started college classes. They said he was planning to work at a halfway house for ex-gang members when he got out, though he hasn't reported for work yet. Does that sound like a killer to you?"

Daniel's mouth flattened. "Definitely sounds strange, Lola. But he was here tonight. Although I'm not sure he didn't try to kill me. Maybe he had Rincon subdued somewhere already."

"Or maybe he wanted you to get Mia Finley out. But you know, the lab found his DNA on the cigarette from the library." She pointed the pen at him. "He was there, too. I'm ninety-nine percent sure he's our guy, but those details are still bugging me. Gotta make it make sense, Junior."

She shoved the pen into her tight gray curls and scratched her scalp with it. "We're going to find Rincon alive. We have to. There are too many pieces here for us not to have a lead." With a brief nod at her partner, Lola walked into the melee of people surrounding Sayers Hall.

A COOL BREEZE BLEW AGAINST Daniel's face, and the tall coconut trees around the building swayed above them, a soothing motion in the midst of chaos. Celia reached for Daniel, her fingers grasping the scratchy brown blanket some paramedic had wrapped around his bare shoulders while he'd been searching for her. "Do you really think Marco won't kill him right away? I don't understand…." Then Celia stopped midsentence as she apparently realized exactly what Marco would do.

Torture, the autopsy report had read, according to Lola. He'd burned them with cigarettes and lighters before dousing them with gasoline and dropping the Molotov cocktail at their feet. No doubt, mental torture played a big part in Sanchez's games, too.

Daniel didn't want to tell Celia. Didn't want to tell her any of it. But she insisted, and so, when Lola walked away to talk to Mia about what she'd seen, he did. In as little detail as possible.

Sometimes, his job really sucked. Like when a crime was so brutal, so horrible, there were actually moments where he couldn't detach from it, not even a little. These men hadn't been the nicest people as teenagers, but they'd been his brother's friends, and they'd made a giant effort to clean up and live an honest life as adults. They hadn't deserved that.

When he finished, Celia leaned forward and put her hands lightly on his waist under the blanket, standing on her toes to brush a soft kiss against his cheek. "I can't imagine how you carry such things around with you all the time. The things you see, every day." She shook her head, biting her bottom lip. "Thank you for telling me." She held him for a moment, and something crackled between them, like paper. Pulling her upper body away from his, she looked down at his side and pulled a receipt out of his pocket.

"What's this?" she asked, holding the slip of paper between her finger and thumb. "It has gum on the back, like someone stuck it on you."

Daniel took it from her, holding it up so he could read what it said in the flashing lights from the fire engines and police cars surrounding them. "U-Keep Storage. Says it's in Santa Monica."

"Where did you get this?" she asked. "You're not storing anything there, right?"

He thought back to his run-in with Marco Sanchez. Marco shoving him up against the wall. Marco's meaty forearm against his throat. Something brushing against his waistband, just before he slammed his fist up into Sanchez's jaw.

"He's sending me a message." Something was there, something Marco Sanchez wanted the LAPD and Patricio Rodriguez to find.

He could only hope it wasn't Antonio Rincon's incinerated body.

RECEIPT IN HAND, LOLA and several of the detectives who had come with her to St. X. left for U-Keep. Daniel, on the other hand, remained behind, choosing instead to take Celia back to his apartment after the paramedics had assured him that she'd suffered no serious effects from smoke inhalation. Having seen what Marco Sanchez could do firsthand, Celia was only too glad to have him stay with her, and she went quietly.

They took Celia's car, a sunny-yellow, new Volkswagen Beetle, and zipped through La Brea down Wilshire, past the famous tar pits, until they got to South Fairfax. Celia hooked a right and pulled into the underground parking garage of the La Brea Intercontinental Apartments. Her stomach lurching at the thought of Antonio, of where he might be right at that very moment, Celia remained silent as she pulled her little car into the Intercontinental's guest-parking spot. Together, they took the elevator to Danny's fourteenth-floor apartment, and with a rattle of keys, he unlocked the door and pushed it open so she could step inside for the first time since…in a long time.

The two-bedroom apartment was small but charming, with cream stuccoed walls that had rounded nooks built into them, simulating the interior of an adobe Spanish mansion. One entire wall in the living room was glass, overlooking a nice-size balcony and affording a view of the Hollywood Hills, including the famous white-lettered sign and a sprawl of twinkling lights dotting their surfaces.

Celia stepped away from the window

and took in Danny's apartment. An ugly but functional boxy couch upholstered in a thick brown-and-beige tweed sat in the middle of the living room. That and a rounded wicker chair with a dumpy little cushion were the only pieces of furniture in the entire room, save a thirty-two-inch silver-and-chrome television set, which sat on top of a matching TV stand filled with various electronics. The TV was flanked on either side by the largest speakers Celia had ever seen outside of an eighties heavy-metal-band concert. The only nod to interior design was a plastic hula girl stuck to the top of the television with a suction cup. Celia flicked the doll's skirt with her finger, and the hula girl's hips started to undulate.

"You know, you've had the same apartment since you were nineteen and you couldn't even be bothered to decorate just a little?" she asked. "Dude, buy a plant." The joke felt hollow, but she felt compelled to pull him out of his thoughts, get him to think of something else besides Antonio. *It'll be all right. It'll be all right.*

Danny gave her a sad half smile. "I'm not good at that kind of thing."

"I'll say," a voice said from the kitchen. "That is one fugly couch, *hermano*."

"Patri-ci-o," Danny trilled in his musical, accentless Spanish, giving the three final syllables equal emphasis as a way of greeting his twin brother. "I thought I smelled something in here."

"Yeah, I do smell pretty sweet, huh?" Patricio moved through the kitchen and into the living room. He wore black pants and a fitted gray silk sweater that hugged his broad shoulders and narrow waist. His hair spiked out in all directions as was the up-to-the-minute style for men in Hollywood, contrasting with Danny's close-cropped no-nonsense hair. But other than artfully messy hair and slightly better taste in clothes, Patricio and Danny were mirror images of each other. Celia had always been able to tell them apart, though, even when they'd tried to fool her. Something in the eyes.

Patricio practically did a double take when he finally noticed her. "Celia?" he said, his golden eyes widening in surprise. "What are...?" Shaking himself, Patricio stepped forward, planting a gentle kiss of greeting on her cheek. "It's good to see you, *querida*. It's been too long."

Though he tried to be subtle, she could practically feel him bugging his eyes out in question at Danny over the top of her head. And she knew the fact that she was covered in soot, wearing only a stained silk bathrobe and a blanket, had little to do with his surprise.

"It's good to see you, too," Celia responded, and she meant it. Though he'd been seriously messed up while she and Danny were dating, Patricio had a warmth and an innate goodness beneath his tough-guy exterior that she'd always adored. It hadn't been his fault that his brother was emotionally closed off, and she'd never held any of that against him. No one had been happier than she when she'd heard Patricio had left the Cobras, happier still when she'd learned he'd joined Danny at night school, both of them getting their bachelor's in criminal justice.

The moment she'd seen him, though, all she could think about was the errand on which he and Joe had gone on to Seattle. She tried to think of a tactful way to broach the subject, then was just going to blurt out the question, tact be damned, but Danny beat her to it.

"Sabrina?" was all he said.

Patricio closed his eyes briefly, and then he shook his head. "It wasn't her," he said softly. The two brothers just looked at each other, their silence speaking volumes, and Celia's heart broke for them. She tugged the blanket tighter around her shoulders, feeling strangely hollow.

Patricio flicked at an imaginary piece of dust on the counter that separated the kitchen from the living room area. "She was the right age, but we knew the minute we saw her that she wasn't our sister. Oh, we asked her, anyway," Patricio responded quickly, anticipating Danny's question. "But her name at birth was Martina, and her adoptive parents changed it to Sabrina. Blond hair, blue eyes. She didn't look a thing like us."

Danny's eyes grew dull with disappointment, and Celia would have given anything to take some of that away, to find Sabrina herself. He nodded. "I'm glad you went, Rico."

Patricio opened his mouth to say something else, but was interrupted by the shrill ring of Danny's cell phone.

"Rodriguez," Danny said, a little more gruffly than usual as he flipped it open. Patricio and Celia watched Danny while he listened to someone talking on the other end for a few seconds, then scowled and headed into one of the back bedrooms.

"Something to drink?" Patricio asked when his brother closed the bedroom door.

Celia shook her head, and the two of them sat on Danny's ugly couch.

"You know," Patricio said, "my last memory of our parents, our birth parents, was Danny and I going to the store with our dad to buy Mami a birthday present. Danny picked out the most hideous orange-flowered couch for her, and the more I told him it looked like something a cat had coughed up, the more he insisted she had to have it. Unfortunately, he got his knack for picking out clothes and furniture from our father, so we actually bought the thing." He laughed, a low, rumbling sound, as he thumped the brown-and-beige tweed with the back of one hand. "Some things never change."

Before Celia could do more than smile in response, the bedroom door swung open and Danny reentered the room. He'd washed his face and had pulled on a navy-blue T-shirt and a clean pair of jeans. "The storage guy won't let Lola search the premises without a warrant," he explained, grabbing his keys off the counter where he'd tossed them. "I have to go see a judge who won't mind being pulled out of bed to get one."

He stopped in front of Celia, tipped her chin with the crook of his finger. "The judge lives two buildings down from me. It's faster if I go," he explained, though Celia didn't miss the flicker of guilt in his eyes.

"It's okay," she said. "Patricio is here. I'll be fine."

Patricio nodded. "Sure, man. Go. I'll keep watch over her."

Danny dropped his hand. "There are some of your clothes in the closet from—" He cut himself off with a glance at his brother. "Last time," he finished.

As soon as he'd left, Celia showered and changed into a soft pair of old Lucky jeans and a burgundy button-down shirt, which she left hanging loose at the waist. A little digging in Danny's closet turned up a pair of platform sneakers, and she slipped those on her feet. When she returned to the living room, Patricio turned his gaze—identical almost to Danny's and Joe's—on her, and whatever it was he was about to say, she knew she wasn't going to like it.

"So what are your intentions toward my brother?" He grinned amiably at her, but she could see he wasn't joking.

Celia headed for the hideous couch, sitting down and leaning back into the cushions. It was ugly, but she had to admit, sinking into it felt divine. Danny always had been a function-over-form kind of guy. "I don't know, Rico," she said, the childhood nickname falling off her tongue before she could stop it. Fortunately, Patricio didn't seem to mind or even notice. "I wish I knew."

"He's falling for you again," Patricio replied. He stared out the window at the city lights below.

She wished she could believe him, could feel secure in knowing what was going on inside that head of Danny's. "How do you know?"

"I know him." Not one to use excessive words, Patricio cut right to the quick of his argument. "You need to figure this out. Both of you."

Oh, yeah, they did. Celia nodded in agreement. All this time. All these years. Every time she saw him, she kept coming back to Danny, as inevitable as the Pacific tide. And somehow, this time, when she was confronted by his mortality and her own again and again, things had changed. She'd always felt immortal, practically, but now... Life was too short to behave the way she and Danny were behaving. Because it had taken only eleven years for her to figure out that hiding behind her old hurts wasn't going to make her happy. Only Danny could do that.

Leave it to her to need a homicidal maniac to put everything into perspective. She took a deep breath, finally ready to admit it out loud. "I think I love him, Patricio. All over again."

But could it work? Would she ever be able to handle a man who closed down as completely as Danny could whenever things got rough?

Patricio put a warm, comforting hand on her shoulder before moving into the kitchen to raid Danny's refrigerator. Snapping open a can of root beer, he walked back into the living room. He held the can out in tacit invitation, but Celia shook her head, so he took a long swallow out of it himself. "Then, *querida,* I think the rest of it will work itself out. He's trying, you know."

"I know." And truly, this time she did.

Just as Patricio took another swig of soda, Danny's telephone rang. With a grimace of disgust, he set the can down and yanked the cordless handset off the base, hitting the on button. "Rodriguez," he said, so like his brother.

"Yeah…yeah, sure. Be right down." Pressing the off button, he tossed the phone back in its place. "Building security. I have to move my car. I could have sworn I put it in one of the guest spots." He tugged his keys out of the front pocket of his pants, tucking the lining back inside when some of it escaped with them. "Want to come?"

Celia shook her head. "I'll be fine. I'll lock the door behind you."

Patricio nodded and then he was out the door, leaving her alone in the apartment with her admission that she'd fallen back in love with Danny still hanging in the air.

Well, what of it? She'd been hanging on to old hurts for so long, maybe it was time to let them go. And if she couldn't get over Daniel Rodriguez and walk away, then maybe it was just time to start all over again and see if they couldn't build something better this time.

She unlatched the balcony door and stepped outside, letting the nighttime breeze lift her hair and cool her skin. Somewhere out in that city, Danny was getting a warrant, and then he'd be coming back to her. And she'd be waiting for him.

Behind her, she heard a rattle of keys, and then the front door swung open. She turned to greet Patricio as he walked back inside.

But it wasn't Patricio who'd come in.

"Oh, my God," she whispered when she realized who it was—a face out of memory from a long time ago. And then she saw the gun.

THE MINUTE DANIEL HANDED the warrant to Lola on the grounds of the U-Keep Storage facility, the entire Homicide Special contingent surrounding her sprang into action. Lola smacked the key on the counter before the recalcitrant manager and demanded to know to which unit it belonged. He grudgingly led them out to unit number 41, and Detectives Donovan and Freeman unlocked the corrugated steel door and rolled it above their heads.

The first thing they noticed was that there was no sign of Rincon. The unit was mostly empty, although one sweep of Donovan's flashlight uncovered definite scorch marks in the center of the concrete floor. Shattered bits of warped green glass lay scattered about the floor, along with bits of telltale cotton. Sanchez had brought his victims here and had dropped his lethal Molotovs at their feet. And, since steel and concrete didn't burn easily, the fire consumed what did—the victims.

Donovan swabbed some of the soot on the ground, while Freeman collected the glass with a pair of sharp tweezers. Lola surveyed the unit with her sharp, beady eyes.

"I'd say we found our crime scene, Junior."

"Looks like."

Though he was itching to stay, to process the scene with Lola like he had hundreds of others, amassing enough evidence to put Sanchez behind bars for the rest of his miserable life, Daniel left the scene. He had to get back to Celia. Fortunately, Freeman and

Donovan were the best of the best, and he had no doubt they'd do an excellent job in his absence. He got into his car and turned the ignition.

As soon as Daniel pulled into his garage, he saw the body, sprawled halfway in, halfway out of the stairwell door.

Screeching to a halt at an awkward angle in the center of the garage, Daniel barely registered putting the car in Park. He threw open the door and lunged out, but something held him pinned to his seat.

With a volley of Spanish curses, Daniel fumbled for the seat belt latch, finally releasing himself, and then he was running to the body on the ground. The first thing he noticed was the man's spiky hair, his gray sweater.

Patricio. Oh, God, no, not Patricio.

He was lying so still. Daniel's hands started to shake violently as he reached for his brother, so afraid, his skin prickled with a cold, clammy sweat. He touched the base of Patricio's throat with two fingers.

Warm skin. A pulse.

Gracias a Dios.

Taking his fingers off of Patricio's throat, Daniel shielded his face with his hand, his breath coming out in shuddering gasps. He squeezed his eyes shut for a moment, pinching the bridge of his nose as he tried to bring himself under control. Patricio needed him. He had to see how badly his brother was injured.

He moved so he could see his brother's face, one cheek resting on the step outside the stairwell doorway. Gingerly, he ran his hands along the back of Patricio's skull, finding, as he thought he might, a large swelling bump where he'd been hit from behind.

Daniel smacked Patricio lightly on the face, trying to bring him back to consciousness. "Rico," he said. "Wake up. Come on."

After what seemed like hours, though probably only five minutes passed, Patricio's eyelids fluttered. "Wha-hmmph?" he murmured.

"Patricio, come on. Wake up," Daniel said.

"Daniel?" Placing his palms flat on the ground beneath his shoulders, Patricio slowly moved himself up into push-up position, and then he wobbled. Daniel reached out and steadied him, helping him get into a seated position. God, he'd never seen his tough-guy brother, bodyguard to the stars, look so pale, so fragile. He never cared to see it again.

"What happened?" Daniel asked.

"I don't know. Someone called me, asking me to move my car, so I came down, and then..." He flipped a palm in the air to demonstrate that he wasn't entirely sure what had happened next. "I didn't even see him coming. I'm usually better than that." He reached back and touched the back of his head. "Ow!"

"What about Celia?" Danny asked, dreading the answer.

"Cel—" Bracing one hand on the cinder-block wall, Patricio lurched quickly to standing. "Oh, Jesus."

Daniel pounded on the elevator buttons, and when the doors didn't open right away, turned and ran up the stairs. He made short work of all fourteen floors, but as soon as he burst into the hallway on his floor, he knew he was too late. The door to his apartment stood wide open.

"Celia!" he called, his heart in his throat as he ran into his apartment. But, as he'd feared, she didn't answer him.

And then his cell phone rang.

Chapter Fourteen

"Rodriguez," Daniel said as he answered his phone.

"Detective Rodriguez?" a woman's voice asked in a soft whisper. When Daniel confirmed his identity, she continued, but her words sounded as if she were speaking through cotton.

"I can't hear you," he said. "Can you speak up?" It wasn't Celia, that he knew, but something about her voice was familiar, even muffled as it was.

"I am Maribel Sanchez." Ah, yes, the lilting Spanish accent of Marco Sanchez's mother. And then another muffled phrase.

"What?" With Celia missing and Marco on the loose, he knew Maribel might hold the key to finding both. But only if he could get her to speak loud enough for him to understand her. "I can't hear you," he ground out, frustrated and nearly shaking with pent-up energy that he had no place to direct.

"I am with Marco," she responded in a harsh whisper. "You must come. I think he is going to hurt us."

"Us?" Daniel's heart skipped a beat. "Where are you? Who's there with you?"

"A woman," Mrs. Sanchez said. "With curly black hair. And a man. I'm not sure where we are, but we're near the water. In a warehouse. It smells like fish."

A lot of places near the water smelled like fish. He needed more. "Can you tell me anything else?" His voice had grown loud and impatient, and he made an effort to calm himself down. "Landmarks you saw on the way over? Anything you see now?"

"I don't know. I—" She stopped talking, and he heard voices in the background. "We drove toward San Pedro, and then we went across a large green bridge to an island. There are many—how you say?—warehouses and ugly little boats."

The Vincent Thomas Bridge. She was on Terminal Island, an artificial island off the coast of San Pedro, about twenty miles south of downtown L.A. Terminal Island served as a major shipping port, not just for the city, but for the whole United States. "I know where you are," he said. "Mrs. Sanchez, we'll be there as soon as possible. Try to stall your son."

"Look for a blue pickup truck outside one of the warehouses. That is where we are." Mrs. Sanchez paused. "He is coming," she said rapidly. "Hurry, *por favor.*" She cut off the connection.

Daniel immediately called Lola and briefed her on the phone call. As he snapped the phone shut, he turned to Patricio.

"Need backup?" his brother asked quietly, his face still drawn and pale from the thump to the head he'd recently suffered.

"You sure? You don't look so good, *hermano,*" Daniel replied, his mind on Celia. Panic and fury squeezed the air out of his chest, making him dizzy, making him gasp. If that bastard hurt Celia, he'd pay.

"I'm fine. It's just a flesh wound," Patricio muttered. "And we're closer to Terminal Island than Lola is," he added.

True. It wasn't as if Patricio wasn't a trained security expert. As far as backup went, there wasn't anyone Daniel would rather have with him. And with or without backup, he was going after Celia. "Okay, let's roll." The two brothers ran to Patricio's Pontiac.

AFTER CROSSING THE Vincent Thomas Bridge behind a convoy of semitrucks, Daniel slowed the car as the wheels rolled onto Terminal Island.

If Los Angeles proper was all bright colors and beautiful people, this was where the city kept its ugly. The island was all corrugated metal and oily, dust-covered glass, dirty asphalt and cracked concrete—none of it flattered by the pale sunrise behind it. Warehouses, tuna canneries and loading docks as far as the eye could see.

Daniel drove toward Fish Harbor, where rusted commercial fishing boats floated on brown water with a light film of oil gracing the top. Rusted loading cranes and giant metal containers dotted the rest of the island's shoreline visible from their car. Despite the ocean breeze, even the air felt thick and gray, laden with dirt and diesel fumes.

"Yuck," Patricio said.

"Yeah."

Daniel wished he could have gotten more information out of Mrs. Sanchez, but her "ugly little boats" comment made him automatically think she must be near Fish Harbor. He slowed the car down to a crawl, and he and Patricio scanned every visible stretch of asphalt for a blue pickup. Daniel's cop sense took over, and he was able to direct all of his focus at finding Mrs. Sanchez, finding Celia. But deep in the back of his mind, he knew how close Celia was to death right now, and the knowledge made him feel a fear so intense, he had to push it away.

"There!" Patricio sat forward in his

chair, the seat belt pulling against his chest, and tapped on the passenger-side window. "Oh, crap, man, sorry. It's black, and not even a truck."

Daniel clenched the steering wheel with both hands, and he could feel his jaw tightening to the point where he was probably in danger of cracking a tooth. Or several.

"We'll find her," Patricio murmured, still scanning the surrounding area. A flock of seagulls glided overhead, and the smell of dead fish seemed to grow more pungent.

"Here." Daniel lifted himself away from the backrest and pulled his cell phone out of his pocket, handing it to his brother. "In case she calls again."

"Now, here's what's funny, dude. Why would Marco want to hurt his own mother?" Patricio craned his neck to get a better view of a parking area behind a tuna cannery, his voice so quiet, it was hard to hear him over the sound of diesel engines and shrieking seagulls. "Especially if his sister's death is what set him off. You'd think his family would be important to him."

Daniel told him about the bruises he'd seen on Maribel's arms, her statement that she was afraid of her sons. "She's been through a lot, I think. A widow, trying to raise two gangbanger sons. I think they take a lot of their issues out on her."

"Whoa." Patricio jerked his head around to stare at Daniel. "She's not a widow."

A beat passed, and then Daniel stomped on the brakes, his involuntary movement causing the car to lurch forward as it stopped suddenly. With an apologetic glance at Patricio, he lifted his foot off the brake and drove forward once more. "What? How do you know?"

"She and her husband divorced a few months after Marco went to prison," Patricio said. "He lives in Fresno."

"And you know this because...?"

Patricio turned away once more, gazing out at their dismal surroundings. "I sent money to her after Sonia died. Anonymously. Sort of checked up on her from time to time." Suddenly, he sat up with a quick movement, and Daniel saw what his brother was looking at before Patricio could say another word.

Parked alongside a nondescript warehouse, in a shadowy corner where they'd almost missed it, was a blue Dodge pickup, looking shiny and out of place. Daniel pulled the car to a halt.

HER HEAD THROBBED WITH a pain worse than any she'd ever felt, and Celia fought to stay asleep, closing her eyes, relaxing her body. But her hands were pinned at an awkward angle behind her back, causing her shoulders to ache and her fingers to tingle, and her head... Oh, God, her head.

Unable to remain blissfully unaware of her physical state, she tried to open her eyes, her head lolling slowly back and forth as if she were a bobblehead doll with a rusty neck joint. She managed to crack one eye open, the other apparently being glued shut.

The first thing she noticed was the dust particles, dancing in the stringy beams of early morning light that leaked through the slats of a boarded-up window. The rest of the room was enveloped in murky darkness. The pungent odor of gasoline filled her nostrils, and across the room...

Celia blinked her good eye, trying to adjust to the darkness. She tried to move her hands, but they wouldn't budge, and she felt a tightening around her wrists, as if someone had tied them behind her back. She tried to move her legs, but they were held immobile as well.

And then it all came back in a rush. Daniel's apartment. Patricio going downstairs. Someone who wasn't Patricio coming back into the apartment, rushing toward her. After that, she remembered nothing.

Across the dingy room, a small flame flickered, grew brighter, and then was snuffed out. Then it flickered again, grew brighter, and then was snuffed out. Someone had a lighter.

And she was tied to a chair, covered in gasoline.

She struggled against her bonds, but they only pulled tighter. "What do you want?" she asked the person across the room. But she knew what they wanted. Oh, how she knew.

She heard a tiny click as the person flicked the lighter on one last time. The flame moved closer, the shadowy presence holding it walking slowly toward her. And that's when Celia started to scream.

"OH, DON'T WORRY, *NENA*." Maribel Sanchez stepped into the thin light afforded by the boarded-up window, holding the lighter in front of her. In her other hand, she held a glass wine bottle with a rag wrapped around the top. "It will only hurt for a few minutes. Just until the top layers of your skin burn off, along with the nerve endings."

"You sick, twisted—" Celia jerked her body, trying to free herself.

"Now, now." Maribel clicked off the lighter with her thumb, tucking it into the pocket of her jeans. "I'd be nice if I were you. Not that it will help."

"Why are you doing this? Where's Marco?" Celia wondered if her stalling question was just prolonging the inevitable. Would Daniel find her? Would anyone find her? And what could they do if they did? One toss of that lighter, and she'd be dead or horribly disfigured, at best. But all Celia knew was that she wanted to live, needed to live, needed to see Daniel again. But if she didn't, she wanted him to know that she'd tried.

Maribel smiled sadly. "Marco, that stupid boy. He doesn't have the guts to do what he promised when his sister died. And it was his fault, he and Paco, running with those gangs until she wanted to join, too. I was a good mother. I raised them to be better."

"He wasn't helping you?" Celia asked.

"Pah," she spat. "He was trying to stop me, the coward. Never could get anything right. I took his cigarette and left it in your library, hoping the police would do the DNA on it and think he did it. Fortunately, I succeeded."

She crouched down at Celia's feet, putting a slim hand on Celia's knee. "You never had a daughter," she said softly. "Sonia was *mi vida, mi corazon*." My life. My heart. "She was beautiful, and so smart. She wanted to be a doctor when she grew up, she said, so she could take care of her father and me when we grew old, and keep us alive forever."

"She sounds like a wonderful girl," Celia murmured, though she suspected Sonia hadn't been the perfect daughter Maribel held her up to be, having tried to get in a gang and all.

Maribel nodded enthusiastically. "*Sí*, she was. So now you see why I have to do this?" Standing once more, she tucked her fingers into the pocket with the lighter, fishing it out.

No, not like this. Don't let it be like this. "Um, no, I don't." Celia did her best to remain calm, to keep Maribel talking, but she really wanted to scream her fool head off and hope someone would come in time. Then she remembered—one toss of the lighter, with or without the bottle. They'd never come in time.

"I have to, for Sonia. She would want the boys who hurt her to hurt." Maribel brought a closed fist over her heart. "I want those boys to hurt. I need them to hurt. So many years, and it doesn't go away, that pain of losing your child."

Using her fingernails to pick at the scratchy twine that bound her wrists, Celia nodded slowly. "I can't imagine what you feel. But why would you want to make the police think Marco was behind this? He's your son."

Maribel's eyes widened. "He should pay! He needs to pay for leading Sonia down that path. It's not my fault! Besides—" she lowered her voice conspiratorially "—it was his idea. That day in the courtroom, when your father let the last of the men that killed my daughter go free."

Celia heard someone shout, and then a small explosion roared from the other end of the warehouse. Flames engulfed the doorway, seeming to move quickly along the wall and up a wooden support.

DANIEL YANKED THE KEYS out of the ignition and ran out of the car, leaving the driver's-side door gaping open behind him. Footsteps behind him, slipping on the gravel coating the crumbling concrete driveway told him Patricio was right behind him. He tugged his gun out of his shoulder holster and clicked off the safety, raising it to face level, barrel pointing upward. As he approached the door, his eyes flicked back and forth, examining each of the dirt-caked windows on the front of the building. He could see no movement behind them.

Patricio moved to the hinged side of the front door of the warehouse, and Daniel took the other side. He listened for a moment, and after hearing nothing, the two of them moved around the building. They didn't need to speak, taking nonverbal cues from each other and assessing the situation. Near one of the windows in the back, he heard voices, and he motioned to Patricio to listen, too. One of the voices sounded like Celia's.

His chest tightening with relief, Daniel motioned to his brother to follow him back to the front of the building. It was quiet there, so chances were, they could enter without being seen.

When they reached the door, Patricio and Daniel flanked the door one more time. At Daniel's nod, Patricio reached over and pulled it open. Daniel moved forward, not noticing the trip wire stretched across the bottom of the doorway until it was much too late.

FIRE, ONLY A FEW YARDS AWAY, and here she sat, immobilized and covered in gasoline. The explosion hadn't taken the building, thank God, but she was terrified to find out what or who had set it off.

"What was that?" Celia cried, a bubble of hysteria rising in her throat despite her best efforts to remain calm.

Maribel smiled at her, still clutching her lighter and wine bottle, gasoline sloshing around inside. "Oh, that was your boyfriend, the detective."

Celia's stomach constricted and her body grew cold. Maribel's voice sounded far away, as if she were speaking through a tunnel.

"I called and invited him here. He gave me his number, you know." Maribel's casual tone made it sound like she was talking about the weather. "I should finish with you quickly, so I can watch him burn and then move on to the next one."

Maribel's eyes darted to the side, and Celia could see Antonio Rincon lying on the floor, unconscious but still breathing. *Daniel. Oh, God, Daniel. Did you know? Did you see it coming? Please, please let him have sensed the trap.* But even as she prayed, she wondered how Danny could have known. They'd been so sure it was Marco.

"I've been planning this for so long." Looking down at the lighter as if she'd just discovered it, Maribel smiled softly and flicked it on with her thumb. "Your father is dead, so you will take his place."

Everything, every sound, every sight, every breath of Celia's coalesced into a piercing awareness of the small flame Maribel held so close to her. She took a shuddering breath in, and the sound roared in her ears. She wondered if it would be her last. *Please, let Danny be okay.*

Celia looked Maribel directly in the eyes. "I'm someone's daughter, too," she said, holding the woman's gaze. "You're doing the same thing to my mother that the leader of the Cobras did to you."

Maribel faltered, and the lighter sputtered and its flame went out. She was silent for a moment, and then a slow smile spread across her aged but still pretty face. "You know what my maiden name is?" Maribel whispered. "Cienfuegos—Spanish for a hundred fires. That's what you and your father and those *bastardos* who killed my daughter are going to burn in when you reach hell. But I have to send you there first. For my daughter."

She flicked the lighter once more, adjusting it so the flame burned nearly two inches high.

"For my daughter."

Her arm came down toward Celia.

"I was the best marksman in my class at the academy, Señora Sanchez," a voice called from behind them. "You don't want to move that flame any closer."

"DANNY!" CELIA CALLED, relief evident in her voice.

"No," Daniel lied, keeping Maribel Sanchez's head in his sights, his focus sharp, his voice deadly. "I'm Patricio. One of the men on your list, Maribel. You don't want me to kill you before you've had the chance to get us all, do you?"

He hadn't been at all surprised to see Maribel Sanchez in the warehouse instead of Marco. Patricio's words about Maribel not being a widow as she'd claimed had made all the discrepancies, all the details that didn't fit shift into place. The seven bottles he remembered on her windowsill corresponded to the seven remaining people she blamed for Sonia's death. The bruises on her arm were marks Daniel himself had put there, the night she'd attacked him on the catwalks at the St. X theater. She'd been the "janitor" he'd seen exiting the gym after telling firefighters where to find McManus. And the shadowy figure Celia had seen on the stairs while Marco himself was on the other end of the building had been Maribel Sanchez. Marco had been trying to rescue Mia that night, prevent his mother's rampage. Marco had been sending a message the only way his conflicted soul knew how.

"I'll burn her!" Maribel spun around,

putting Celia between herself and the gun. She held her Molotov cocktail in one hand, the still-lit lighter in the other. "I swear to God, I will."

Daniel stepped closer, the gun still aimed at her head. He kept his mind blank. Nothing took his focus, nothing made him falter. Just him, her and the Glock in his hand, ready to tear her apart, "If you do," he said softly, "I will blow your freaking head off before you can take another breath."

Maribel screamed with a rage and a grief that was terrifying to watch. "You killed my daughter!" Sudden tears ran down her face. "She was the most beautiful little girl, and you murdered her with your bare hands, with this!" She shook the bottle violently, and its lethal mixture of gasoline and soap sloshed around inside. He remembered that one of the Cobras had delivered the death blow to Sonia using a broken bottle. "You deserve to die! You deserve to burn!"

A shot rang out, and the bottle shattered in Maribel's hands. She screamed again, opening her palm, and glass rained down on the ground.

Patricio stepped out of the shadows to Daniel's left, having delivered the shot that destroyed her weapon. He, too, held a gun aimed for Maribel. "It's over, Maribel," he said. "I'm sorry."

Daniel wondered what his brother was apologizing for.

Just then, the LAPD SWAT team burst through the doors, dressed in black and wearing face shields and body armor. They took Maribel into custody, leaving Daniel to release Celia from her bonds.

Using a pocketknife he carried on his key chain, Daniel quickly sliced through the twine that bound Celia's hands and feet.

"Daniel," she said, gasping his name, touching his face, wincing as she turned his head to examine the bleeding cut and scrape on his cheek. "I thought she'd killed you."

"She nearly did," he said, loving the feel of her hands on him. "I had to dive onto my face to avoid her homemade bomb."

"But it—"

"Exploded?" he finished. "Yeah, Patricio knows how to set those off without hurting himself."

She shook her head, and for once she was speechless. And then she was in his arms, and the terrible emptiness he'd felt, he'd made himself feel as he'd confronted Maribel, vanished, and in its place was the knowledge that he'd almost lost his girl. "Celia," he murmured, closing his eyes, burying his hands in her glorious hair. "Celia."

They remained like that for several minutes, just holding each other while Daniel tried to get back some of the detachment that had allowed him to face Maribel without crumbling. He didn't want to stop feeling what he felt for Celia—he just wanted to be able to speak.

"Daniel." Celia leaned back, still in the circle of his arms, still running her hands across his body as if unable to believe he was there. "I have to tell you—"

"Shh, baby girl," he said. "I have something to say first." Putting everything into words was harder than he'd thought, but he'd be damned if he'd say the wrong thing this time. So he pulled Celia close and murmured into her ear.

"I love you," he said. "I might not always say the right things, and God knows I don't always do the right things, but that has been a constant in my life since you walked into it. I love you. I'm sorry I ever closed down and shut you out, and if you let me, I'll spend the rest of my life learning to be what you want me to be."

He took a deep breath and pulled back so he could see her face. "You said I only told you you were beautiful when I wanted to sleep with you." He stopped and looked away for a moment, then turned his gaze back on her. "I should have told you all the damn time."

Reaching up, he cupped her face with the palm of his hand. "If you walk away from us again, Celia Inez, know this—every day, every damn time I hear a tango or see a red dress or hear someone wobbling around in a pair of ridiculous shoes,

I will think of you. I will wish you were with me. And I will love you until I die."

Celia just stared at him when he finished. And then she burst into tears.

"Uh…" Daniel let her head fall on his shoulder, rubbing her back as he pondered his sheer helplessness when confronted with a crying woman. "Is this bad?"

Celia put her slim hand on his chest, looking at her fingers as she took deep, shaking breaths, trying to bring herself under control. And, thank the Lord, she was smiling. Still crying, too, but a smile had to be good.

She turned her gaze upward, on his face, and hiccupped. "Wow," she said.

"Yeah." He smiled back at her, feeling a little surprised himself.

Another hiccup, and then a delicate snort, if there was such a thing. "That was impressive, Holmes."

"Yeah?" His smile grew wider.

"I wanted to tell you—" hiccup "—to tell you how much…" She bent her head and swiped at her eyes. "I love you, Danny. So much. I'm so sorry for everything, for all the stupid things I said and did over the past few years—"

"Shh." He put his finger over her lips. "Say the first part again."

Sniff. "I love you?"

"Yeah, that part." He took her in his arms and kissed her softly. "That's all we need to know, baby girl."

Epilogue

Marco Sanchez was cleared of all charges, and Maribel Sanchez pleaded guilty to two counts of arson and three counts of murder—in the second degree, a plea bargain in exchange for her guilty plea. But the likelihood of it all was she'd spend the rest of her life in prison. A more immediate consequence of Maribel's arrest was that Lola finally stopped calling Daniel "Junior."

Marco and his brother Paco went to work for the Carlos Rivera Halfway House for youth who used to be in gangs, both men determined to do something good with their sister's memory, after so many years of ugliness.

Though they hadn't found Sabrina, Joe, Daniel and Patricio continued their search, determined to reunite their broken family once and for all. But even with their baby sister still missing, they all got together, one warm June night that was almost perfect.

They sat around a white linen-covered table at Ca'Brea, Celia's favorite restaurant—Daniel with Celia, Joe with his fiancée Emma, Patricio and their parents, Felicia and Edgardo Rodriguez. Candles flickered under glass fairy lamps, and Daniel stood, raising his glass of wine to the love of his life.

"Celia, I have waited for I don't know how many years to tell you…" Daniel stopped. "I mean, I just wanted to say…" Say what? Why couldn't he just say it.

God, flowery speeches were so not him.

He stole a glance at Celia, who waited expectantly, her eyes sparkling in the candlelight. And he knew, at that moment, that they'd put the past behind them, that they loved each other with everything they had.

"I can't do this," he finally said. "I was going to give you this great speech but—" He fished a ring box out of his pocket, a brilliant ruby with diamonds all around— no plain white rocks for his girl. "Marry me?"

"Oh, Danny." Celia covered her mouth with her hands and then pushed her chair away from the table. She jumped up to standing, the skirt of her red dress swirling around her incredible legs, and threw her arms around him.

"Is that a yes?" he asked.

"How about a 'Yes', right now?"

"Uh…" Across the table, Joe cleared his throat. "I'm not sure what California law states about that. You might need a blood test." Emma hit him in the ribs with a sharp elbow, and with an "oof," he fell silent.

Celia just laughed, her wonderful, musical laugh. "I don't care if we have to fly to Fiji. Let's do it. We can have the big, froufrou wedding later." She cupped her hand around Danny's cheek, and her boundless energy became subdued as she looked into his eyes. "I let you get away too many times, Daniel Ramon Rodriguez. I'm not about to be that stupid again."

Overcome with emotion, Daniel leaned forward and kissed her soundly.

"Vegas?" he murmured against her mouth when they came up for air, the hoots and applause of their family ringing in their ears.

"Church of Elvis?" She grinned and kissed him again.

"You got it, baby girl."

And Patricio, Felicia, Edgardo, Joe, Emma, Celia and Daniel filed out of the restaurant and piled into their cars, on their way to Vegas and the rest of their lives.

* * * * *

Don't miss Patricio Rodriguez's story when
the MISSION: FAMILY *miniseries continues next month with*
SHADOW GUARDIAN,
only in Harlequin Intrigue!

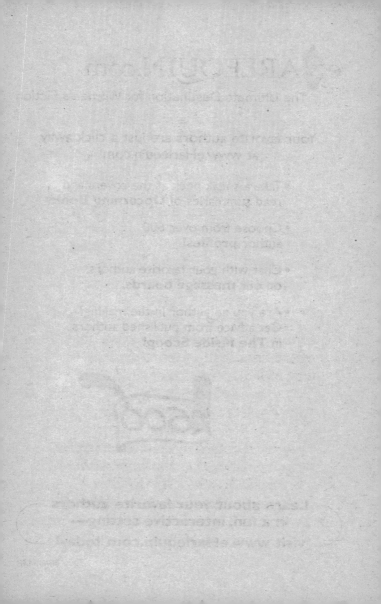

Silhouette®

SPECIAL EDITION™

Emotional, compelling stories that capture the intensity of
living, loving and creating a family in today's world.

Desire

Modern, passionate reads that are powerful and provocative.

INTIMATE MOMENTS™

Romances that are sparked by danger and fueled by passion.

SILHOUETTE Romance

From today to forever, these love stories offer
today's woman fairytale romance.

BOMBSHELL

Action-filled romances with strong, sexy, savvy women who save the day.